RAIL WALKING

and Other Stories

RAIL WALKING

and Other Stories

LINDA L. DUNLAP

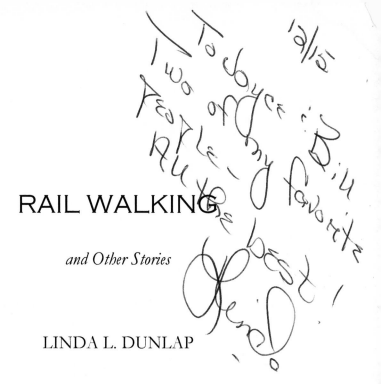

Eudora Publishing

Winter Park, Florida

RAIL WALKING and Other Stories. Copyright © 2015 by Linda L. Dunlap

All rights reserved. Published in the United States of America by Eudora Publishing

"A Crazy Patchwork Quilt" was first published in *Savannah Literary Journal* as "Melissa." "On A Chilly October Afternoon" was first published in *Rosebud*. "Clowns" was first published in *Ithaca Women's Anthology*. "The Tackle Box Files" was first published in *The Louisville Review*. "The Hurting's The Same" was first published in *Old Hickory Review*. "Jacob's Ladder" was first published in *The Black Hammock Review*. "Rail Walking" was first published in *Calliope*. "Goldenrod" and "Scenes From My Study Window" were first published in *Timber Creek Review*. "The Feed Room" was first published in *Southern Exposure* as "The Three of Them and Lucky." "In The Palm Of Mama's Hand" was first published in *The Crescent Review*. "I'm Here, Mr. Sullivan" was first published in *Florida Magazine*. "Intentions" was first published in *New Southerner*.

Cover photograph © Jennifer Reichardt
Cover design © Jessie Compton
Author photo © Michael Wolfson
ISBN-13: 978-0-692-53077-1

To Don, of course, and to Julie, who made it happen

TABLE OF CONTENTS

All human beings are commingled out of good and evil.

Robert Louis Stephenson

RAIL WALKING

THE DAY LUELLEN ran away with the baker, I was perched on the front porch rail with my head between my legs, staring at the world upside down. Everything looked different like that, like a magic rain shower had washed away all the colors on earth and they'd come back brand new. Luellen looked especially different propped against the gatepost next door, searching up and down the street for the baker. She'd piled her hair on top of her head in a jumble of unruly curls. Some loose strands, limp from the staggering summer heat, clung to her neck in damp wisps. Luellen had a particularly high forehead and with her hair pulled away from her face, her eyes shone as saucy and clear as bright green plastic buttons. According to Mama, the forehead came from Luellen being part Indian and Lord only knows where the green eyes came from.

Luellen's suitcase, a pitiful battered thing she'd brought from Atlanta when she married my brother Dock, was hidden under an azalea bush beside the gate. She'd tried so hard to keep me from seeing it, I decided to accommodate her and pretend a ragged corner wasn't sticking out in plain sight from between the crinkly blossoms.

I inched away from her, down the rail to the dining room where Mama had opened the French doors to circulate the breeze.

She was prone to discourage rail walking, so I was careful to stay out of sight. I overheard her inside pointing out the tarnish spots on the flatware to Marcelle, our everyday cleaning lady. "There's a place where your finger is," Mama said.

"Reach me that clean rag," Marcelle answered as though anxious not to miss a speck.

I wasn't fooled. I knew their business in the dining room didn't have one iota to do with tarnish spots. Standing next to the French doors gave them a chance to keep an eye on what was going on next door.

Bending over, I imagined I was glued to the ceiling like a chameleon. Looked at from this view, the impatiens beside the steps, ordinarily a dusty faded rose, took on such a smash of color, the green leaves seemed to disappear entirely and the bush gleamed like a solid ball of fire.

I edged past the corner post. Then tilting my arms back and forth for balance, I waltzed to the end of the porch toward Luellen. At nine years old, I was considered too old for rail walking, but I'd started late. Scabs speckled my arms and legs from where I'd practiced all week.

"You're finally getting the hang of it," Luellen said when I turned around without falling off.

I knew she was trying to attract my attention, but I went on weaving along the rail, acting as if I hadn't heard her. The gate latch made a *click, click* sound when she lifted it and dropped it back into place. She took a deep breath. "Jane Lind, come get Crystal so she can stay with ya'll 'til Dock gets home from the bank," she said.

I missed a step and wound up with one leg dangling. Sitting down carefully, I propped my chin in my palm. A yellow jacket's nest hung from the ceiling like a clump of dusty pipes. I stared up at it. That was the trouble with rail walking—the least thing could break your concentration.

"Now, let me get this straight," I said as if I was carrying on a conversation with the yellow jackets darting about overhead.

"Yesterday you act like you don't ever want me to set foot in your house again. Today you tell me to mind your little girl 'til your husband comes home from work."

I heard the steady *click* of the latch.

"On top of that," I went on. "You tell me I prop the pillows up so high on your bed they look like they're fixing to march off the foot. And . . ." I said in a loud, mean-sounding voice, "I hang your red kimono in the back of the closet facing the wall so you can't locate it, you say." I wanted to make sure Luellen knew how much she'd hurt my feelings yesterday. I was short for my age and couldn't reach across a wide double bed no matter how hard I stretched.

"Jane Lind . . ." she said, rubbing her hand across the rising mound of her stomach.

Mama said Luellen's a Barker from Lower Mill Creek even if she had spent time in Atlanta. Everybody knew what kind of people the Barkers were, moving through downtown Langston like a herd of turtles on a Saturday afternoon in a pick-up loaded to the gills with runny nose children one could easily see suffered harshly from rickets and other ailments of neglect. Mama said Dock married Luellen in the first place to torment her, his own mother, who wants only the best for her children, including him. As far as she was concerned, he'd scraped the bottom of the barrel.

"It's common knowledge at the post office how it was Luellen's idea to move next door," Marcelle told Mama. "Lomus Till says Luellen wants you to be reminded every time you walk out on your front porch that in spite of all you did to keep them apart, she won."

"That riffraff at the post office, including Lomus Till I might add, will go to any lengths to promote family discord."

"Makes a lot of sense if you ask me."

"If I'm not mistaken, Marcelle, nobody did." Mama said some cleaning ladies know their place and some don't. She was forever having to remind Marcelle where hers was.

I didn't know why Dock married Luellen or why they'd moved next door, but I did know Luellen had been acting peculiar lately. She'd totally ignored me since the day a month before when I'd strolled Crystal down to Riggs Soda Fountain and brought her back with a Z-shaped scratch across the side of her face. She'd leaned over to reach for her ice cream cone and toppled out of the stroller.

"What if she'd fallen on her head? Why, the soft spot's not even closed up good yet," Luellen had yelled, jabbing her finger in my face. She was an awful finger pointer when she got mad.

"It's only a little place and I cleaned it off good. Mr. Riggs put some salve on it right away."

Luellen went on and on about how careless I'd been until finally I'd had enough. "You make it sound like I dumped Crystal out of the stroller on purpose, which I did not. And I question the remark about the soft spot," I said. "In case you haven't noticed, Crystal *is* four years old. You think it takes the soft spot forever to close? Even I know better than that!" Grown-ups are famous for giving children credit for having no sense at all.

All the while Luellen yelled at me and I yelled back, I was side-glancing over my shoulder to make sure Mama wasn't around to hear me. I wasn't allowed to sass a grown up—even Luellen.

For the longest time, Luellen behaved as if I'd disappeared from the face of the earth. When she strolled Crystal down the walk, I'd wave like crazy from our front porch, but she never turned an eye my way. As far as she was concerned, I was invisible. I, for one, think acting like a human being isn't there when they are in plain sight is the rudest thing another human being can do.

Then about a month ago, everything changed. Luellen had shampooed Crystal's hair and was sitting on their front steps in the sun for it to dry. When she saw me on our porch, painting my toenails, she called, "Jane Lind, honey, why don't you come play with Crystal?"

I didn't stop to ask myself why she'd changed her mind and had now decided to be nice. I just capped the nail polish and slid it beneath the bougainvillea vine to hide it from Mama, then I dashed across the yard before Luellen could change her mind back. She scooted over to make room for me on the step. Crystal giggled and squirmed, wrinkling her nose like she always did when she's glad to see you.

"Now watch how I fit the strands snug over the curlers at the end," Luellen said while she rolled Crystal's hair. I marveled at how fast she whipped the damp strands up in the little rolls that looked like sausage links. Luellen's real good when it comes to working with hair.

All the encouragement I needed came the next morning when Crystal, her nightgown tangled around her knees, called, "Jane Lind, Mama says to come help me tie my shoes."

After that, I was with Luellen and Crystal from the minute I woke up until I felt my way home through the long spooky shadows that separated our houses at night.

Mama said, "I might as well forget about setting your place at the supper table. You're never here to eat with us anymore."

When Luellen let me make up the bed in the big corner room where she and Dock slept, I began to pretend that her house was mine and Crystal belonged to me.

Then yesterday, I was teaching Crystal to color and stay in the lines when I caught Luellen staring at me like she was mad about something. Finally she said, "You don't know how to do anything right. Those pillows are about to march off the foot of the bed, they're propped so high. And where's my kimono?" She snatched the crayon from my hand.

I was about to say I didn't think the pillows were different from any other day when I noticed how Luellen stood, clutching the crayon so tight her knuckles were white. She covered her face with her hands and started crying out loud hard. "On top of that," she sobbed, "no matter what anybody says, there are just two classes of people, good and bad."

I was the one staring now.

She threw the Crayola across the room as hard as she could. It landed against the windowsill and splinters of purple crayon flew in every direction. She propped her hands on her hips. "And neither one of them has a darned thing to do with which fork you eat your salad with."

Crystal, who'd been filling in the background on a circus tent, closed her coloring book when her mama started yelling. As the crayon bounced off the windowsill, she slid across the slick linoleum floor and hooked her arms around a leg of the kitchen table.

"I'm not surprised," Mama said when I ran home crying. "Now that Luellen's sure you've learned to take care of Crystal properly, you've somehow become part of this awful sin she's committing."

I ran past her without saying a word. Of course, I couldn't feature Mama being much help where Luellen was concerned. They'd hardly exchanged words since Mama told Luellen what color to paint her kitchen—glossy white—and for spite, Luellen painted it blue with eggshell trim on the cabinets and door facing.

Lying upstairs on my bed, I studied the cobwebs Marcelle had missed over the drapes and tried to figure out what was up. Luellen had been so nice to me and now she wasn't again. I wished she'd make up her mind and stick with it so I'd know what to expect. I felt like a yo-yo twirling back and to on its string. And sin! What sin?

Then all of a sudden, it dawned on me. Luellen was running away with the baker. She actually planned to leave Dock and Crystal. For the baker, of all people! He was a queer scarecrow of a man who smelled like vanilla extract and fruitcake and was forever dropping by to see Luellen when Dock was at work. Dock was better looking, even with the drooping eyelid from where the rooster had pecked him when he was ten. Mama said he was lucky he didn't lose half his sight.

On top of that, even though the baker wasn't even a dwarf, he lived in one of the tiny houses on East Paulsen that was built as a winter home for the circus midgets. Luellen wouldn't tell me why he'd do a strange thing like that. In fact, she hardly mentioned him at all except to say that he gave her cinnamon buns at ten percent over cost, which Mama said she found doubtful.

"Jane Lind, Crystal can't stay by herself," Luellen said now like she hated to beg but would if she had to.

I'll never know what Dock ever saw in you, I wanted to shout but didn't when I saw the baker swish around the corner, a white cap crumpled on his head like a mushroom. When Luellen spotted him, she stopped fidgeting with the gate latch, tucked in her blouse and smoothed her skirt down over her hips. Her face broke into a smile, the widest I'd ever seen on her before. Suddenly I knew what it was Dock saw in her. Her eyes began to shine and her face lit up like the biggest present under the Christmas tree had her name on it.

The baker opened the gate, flipping aside the end of a red scarf he wore wrapped like a bandage around his neck. A whiff of fruitcake drifted my way when he swept up her suitcase and bounced it against his knee, waiting.

I grabbed the post, pulled myself up on the rail until I was standing. With the toe of my shoe I beat a *tap, tap* on the banister to remind Luellen I was there to be considered. She glanced over at me like she was surprised to find me still on the planet. Then she jerked her head around, looked me straight in the eye. "I could take her with me."

Easing toward her, I tried to act natural. "You wouldn't do that to Dock. It would break his heart in two."

Luellen stood still as a gravestone in Lottie Nash Cemetery. She knew I'd spoken the truth. She looked down at the ground, stubbed her toe against a clump of Bermuda grass that edged the walk. Her face sagged then like there was something heavy pulling down on each cheek. If she's ever to be sorry for this sin she's in the middle of, it's now, I thought.

She turned and put her hand up to shade her eyes. The chicken pox scar high up on her cheek shone like the head of a ten-penny nail in the bright sunlight. She gazed behind her where Crystal stood inside the screen door, rubbing the fuzzy skin of a peach against the side of her face. Luellen glanced at the baker, then back at Crystal.

The baker tossed his arm across Luellen's shoulder and pulled her close. Smiling, he began to hum softly. For a second, Luellen stood stiffly beside him. Then a tiny smile played across her face as if she recognized the song he was humming. Reaching up, she brushed his cheek with the tips of her fingers. With her eyes still on his, she said, "There's pimento-cheese sandwiches and tea cakes on the back of the stove for supper, Jane Lind. Tell Dock I didn't have a chance to pick up his Ipana. He can have what's left in my tube." Then, with their hands clasped and swinging back and forth between them, Luellen and the baker walked off down the street together.

Limply, I leaned against the post. I hadn't taken a breath for a long time. I figured I'd been fair about it. She could have changed her mind anytime she wanted to. Still, my face felt suddenly hot, like I was coming down with something.

When Luellen and the baker reached the fire hydrant at the end of the street, Mama and Marcelle came through the French doors onto the porch. The only sound was the whispery rustle of the bougainvillea as it stirred in the breeze. Marcelle's mouth was a big gaping O in the middle of her face like she was holding a high note on a hymn in Sunday school. Finally, she clamped her mouth shut and turned to Mama. "There she goes, wearing a striped blouse and plaid skirt after you've gone over it with her time and again."

"Wearing too much lipstick as usual," Mama said slowly, like her mind was on something else. "It comes down to the same thing in the end—some people can't be taught. At least now

Crystal can grow up with some opportunity for refinement. And it's not like Luellen won't have another one to keep her entertained before long."

I didn't think Luellen had on too much lipstick. She wore a new shade, ruby-colored, that would have looked better on me with my light complexion, but it went nicely with the narrow stripe in her blouse. And I'd never thought of Crystal as entertainment. I thought Mama looked for things sometimes.

Marcelle held a salad fork up to the light. "Aren't they a pair?" she asked, waving the fork in the air.

"There's fried chicken and deviled eggs on the bottom shelf of my icebox," Mama said. "*That's* what Dock's having for supper tonight. Luellen's pimento-cheese is much too sweet. Who ever heard of adding sugar?" She talked fast, the words crowding one on top of the other like she wasn't really listening to them. I was reminded of what Luellen told me once. "Nobody says what they really mean at your house, Jane Lind. They're famous for covering the truth up with words."

Crystal hadn't moved from behind the screen door. Juice from the half-eaten peach dribbled down her chin. Any other time she'd bob down the walk dodging the cracks, singing the Popcorn Man song. She'd be four the second Monday in September and had just learned all the words. Now, she didn't make a sound.

"Jane Lind, stop prancing around on that rail and go bring her over here," Marcelle said. "If I don't get that play suit in soak right away, she'll have a stain on it from now on. Peach juice is the mischief to get out of waffle pique."

Crystal tossed the peach pit at me when I reached the steps. I dodged it and leaned against the banister while she marched up and down the porch, muttering, "You're not my mama. You're not my mama."

I waited patiently for whatever she was having to be over with. Her steps slowed finally until she stopped in front of me. She bent over and put her head upside down between her legs.

"I can't see," she whined.

"You can from the rail."

Batting the bright green eyes Crystal had gotten from Luellen, she lifted her arms. "Reach me up."

I struggled with her to the top of the rail, then held my hands around her waist so she wouldn't fall. When she bent down, her curls, tight as corkscrews, draped over and tangled in her fingers. I'd practiced and was good at working with hair now. I thought I'd roll it so the curls wouldn't be so tight from now on.

As Luellen and the baker rounded the corner at the end of the street, a yellow jacket darted down from the ceiling and lit on the back of Crystal's hand. She screamed, tilted off the rail and spilled into my arms. I caught her, twirled her around and around until I was dizzy from the spinning. We dropped to the floor in a hot, sweaty heap.

Mama and Marcelle parted the bougainvillea, peered through to see what the commotion was about. When Mama saw that we weren't hurt, she said, "Young ladies don't parade around on the front porch rail looking at the world upside down with their underpants showing."

I was busy taking care of Crystal or I'd have told her that sometimes the world makes more sense that way.

Rocking Crystal back and forth, I cradled her against my chest. On the back of her neck, the hair was matted almost solid with perspiration. I'd have to put her in the tub and give her a bath before supper, but for now, I'd just sit and hold her.

I'll bet she wouldn't have cried at all if the yellow jacket hadn't stung her.

THE FEED ROOM

I FEEL IT already. Today is guaranteed to be one Samson, the fellow I've been with for a year now, tells me he'd like to be a fly on the wall. He says that about lots of days in the Feed Room. He's right. Stuff is always going on here you wouldn't want to miss.

Penny perches at one end of the counter while Silo props at the other, the two of them like bookends. I've spoken to Penny, pretend I don't see Silo settling Lucky, his blue tick hound, at his feet. Per usual, he totally ignores the *No Pets Allowed* sign beside the door. What does he think, that Lucky is a special breed that's exempt? Every morning we have the same go 'round. Not only is the dog inside when she shouldn't be, but Lucky is a thief. I hate a thief, especially when it's a dog.

I line up the catsup holders on the counter and fill them with the little fat packets that squirt catsup down your shirtfront when you rip off the corner. We've used them since Minnie Roundtree from the We-Kare saw Tan Mason lick his knife and then stick it in a bottle of catsup. Miss Minnie said it turned her stomach. But I wonder about her sometimes. She's been to the Feed Room often enough to know she's not putting her feet under a table at the Waldorf. If you're looking for fancy, you won't find it here. None of those earth colors or deep dark booths for Jack. He took over the Feed Room when Jess, his mother, died. I think he'd have been satisfied to close it down, but everybody made such a fuss. He gives me free rein in running it.

It's a no-frills place, but I keep it bright. The tables are big enough for elbow room with space left over in the center for a potted plant, alive and mainly well. I have a knack. Crystal, my granddaughter, says "Grandma, you can make a pencil grow." I've sprinkled stout hanging baskets about, but nothing to block the sun from coming in sharply through the windows. This leaves in full sight the Chinese restaurant across the street, where green-striped shutters cover a good portion of the dragon curling up in splashy reds and blacks.

The Red Dragon has been in decline since the bus boy disappeared with the rice cooker and Foo Wong served minute rice to the lunch crowd. Something sacrilegious about that. People put it in the same category as the incident with Tan and the catsup bottle. Still, folks on our side of town keep coming to The Feed Room. Either they don't care or being American is easier to forgive.

The breakfast crowd has thinned. Dinkins has picked up Miss Minnie and taken her back to the We-Kare. He brings her over in the van every morning, makeup caked in heavy streaks from her cheeks to her chin. But her forehead is bare as if she's forgotten it's up there. She orders The Deluxe, two eggs over light, toast and a sausage patty—links give her heartburn. I can sympathize. I have stomach trouble and shy away from spicy stuff myself. She comes because she says it's hard to face old man Harley at the nursing home on an empty stomach, watching him fork scrambled eggs into his mouth, missing more often than not. He inserts his dentures when he's done, so other than breakfast, meals at the We-Kare are tolerable.

It's not often the Feed Room is a step up in anybody's estimation, although we do maintain a standard—no dirty talk, no jokes about blacks, Jews, Polacks. Naturally, this eliminates the majority of what some folks consider humorous.

Since the crowd we cater to is more interested in the flavor of the food than which fork to use, nobody looks twice when you put your elbows on the table. *Good Food! Good Service! Cheap!* as the sign says in the window.

Then Miss Minnie gets offended when Tan licks his knife. Go figure.

I stand the catsup packets on their ends like I'm about to shuffle a deck of cards, hear a *chop, chop* sound from the kitchen. Today is Tuesday. Danny is busy dicing onions for the liver special. He's hung over again, slams plates down on the pass-thru with a crash. I thought we'd done something about that, but I see we haven't licked it yet. He's been known to show up with a split lip, a black eye. Lily Rose, his daughter says, "When Daddy starts drinking he thinks he's the U.S. Peacekeeping force."

As I close the shutters across the pass-thru to stifle the clatter and sausage smell, I watch Penny in the mirror over the counter. She blows on her coffee, idly taps a thumbnail on the counter and looks around, surveying the joint. A gold half-heart dangles as innocently as a cross around her neck.

When she pushes back her hair that glistens like an oil slick, I get a view of her busy ears. I see nine—that's nine, I count them myself—earrings dangle from each ear. They dance against her cheek, each earring a string of beads in bright turquoise, rusty terra cotta and shades of copper like wet sand. I like them, picture all those Southwestern colors sweeping against my cheek, each ear a little piece of the Painted Desert.

Then I brush back a strand of my own hair, a faded-out cork shade that I got from my mama. I finger one of my tiny stud earrings and know I lack the courage for anything fancier. Besides, Samson would have a fit.

Penny is early today—and by herself. That's unusual. Recently she and Merle opened an auto repair shop in the old Goodwill Store on the corner of Vine. Ordinarily they close at five, then hightail it here in time for the Blue Plate Special.

Nobody knows where they hail from. At the Feed Room we don't ask, figure if we're supposed to know, we will. Lots of speculation though. They seem honest, did a good job repairing Franklin Pearson's Toyota when he was rear-ended out by the stockyard.

Penny's gaze lights on Silo now and sticks. I can tell she's spotted his nose and is trying to get past it. I want to say, *Honey, I know the feeling.*

Except for the nose, Silo is an ordinary guy with thinning hair. But his nose stretches out in front of him like a freckled flounder, a pale undernourished species with sprinkles of black pepper down both sides. The first time I saw him, his nose stopped me, too. I said to myself, if I was his mama, I don't care how much it cost; that nose would have to be fixed—even if it meant paying it off on an installment plan.

For a while, after he closed his duct-sucking business, Silo worked Layman and Central as a school-crossing guard. At rush hour, his nose backed up traffic as far as the eye could see. But once the initial shock wore off it didn't bother me in the least. It just goes to show how you can get past anything once you set your mind to it.

The whole time Penny stares at him, Silo doesn't look up. He's busy trying to hide Lucky, which is wasted effort. Like I don't know the stupid dog is here.

With a wet rag, I swipe at a stubborn spot of green caked hard on the counter. When it doesn't budge, I scrape at it with my fingernail. It's rough, like cement. Spinach, maybe? Finally it disappears. I catch sight of some crumbs, get rid of them, then feel along the underside of the counter for gum, stuff people like Miss Minnie raise Cain about.

Eventually, my eyes travel back to Penny and the necklace. She doesn't try to hide it. Of course, figuring out where the other half dangles is a no-brainer. The name *Merle,* engraved in sturdy block letters, stares out like it's guarding the down shaft to a gold mine. Most everybody in Lemon City has the scoop on that situation.

It's not the kind of thing seen much in this part of Georgia, in a town as small as ours, but they seem to have pulled it off.

Then I see Silo's face. When he turns, spots Penny, his eyebrows shoot up, stay arched like they're hooked on something overhead. I stand with my mouth half open, think how I'm mistaken about everybody in town knowing, although Samson swears we know such things even when we don't know we know. He says it's just how much we let drift up into our minds at the time. I'm not buying it. I know Silo. He doesn't have a clue.

The look on his face is one I haven't seen since Ruth died five years ago. He closed up like a fist then, sealed the place inside himself where those looks come from, like boarding up a house. Since then, he's walked around, out of step with the world, his shoulders slumped like something heavy is riding them— something he needs to apologize for.

In his grief, Silo's life became divided into Before Ruth and After Ruth. When he lost her, he forgot how the easy back-and-forth that never means much but keeps people connected, works. I think this drove well-wishers away from him more than anything else.

One day Ernest Thomas stopped beside Silo, who slumped on his usual stool at the counter, and slung his arm across Silo's shoulders. "It's cloudy. What do you think, Silo? Will we get a shower today?"

No big deal. Ernest is just being nice, making conversation. Right?

Silo looked up. "You mean outside?"

Ernest's arm fell from Silo's shoulder. Finally he said, "Yeah, Silo, outside." He gave the shoulder a pat and stepped out the door, shaking his head.

After a while, people began to have business elsewhere when they passed Silo's stool. Where before they wanted to help him grieve his loss, they now took to hurrying by without a word. Finally they stopped seeing him all together. They'd have noticed if he wasn't there, but they stopped noticing when he was.

After everybody took to leaving Silo to himself, he came to dote on Lucky more than ever. He'd always been a fool about the dog, but now he seemed to think if he let go of her, he'd lose his grip on life as well. Other than coming here for meals, he spends his time on his front porch with the dog curled in a puddle at his feet. They sit, as lively as doorstops, with their heads cocked to one side like they're listening in on something important, something no one but the two of them can hear, while his bug zapper sends moths and fireflies reeling into forever.

Now, what Silo forgot in those years, he suddenly reinvents in the time it takes him to scoot down the counter and straddle the stool next to Penny. His moves are smooth like he's polished them. This surprises me. I'd have thought when he forgot what being alive was all about, the actions that went along with it would go, too. As he zeroes in on Penny, something hot and proud flashes between them. Quick as a jolt of electricity, I see the fever of life and loving rush back into him.

The fierce new spark in Penny's eyes brings me up short. She got past his nose in record time.

I gaze through the plate glass window. It's windy outside, as only Ground Hog Day in Lemon City can be. Signs slap back and forth like they're carrying on a conversation with each other.

If ever I'm tempted to intervene and say something, it's now. *Silo, there's something you need to know before you get in over your head.* The right words might make a difference. He and Ruth never had children, so no offspring is here to say, *Hey, Pop, I don't think this is such a good idea.*

Ruthie, as she was known back then, played tambourine in the church band. Silo took her out the first time in his daddy's 1956 Nash with the fold-down leather seats, a tiny "s" in the back cushion where, on a trip to the Cyclorama, he'd carved his initial with his new pocketknife. When he parked at the Lemon River Dam with Ruthie, he opened that same knife and cut a Snickers bar square down the middle.

"Take your pick," he said. "I'll be fair with you." And he had been—even though Ruth expected him to make something of himself on the scale of her own daddy who was mayor of Lemon City for 30 years and never got over the fact that Silo hadn't.

"I never let my pride keep me from loving Ruth," he said once, studying the coffee grounds in the bottom of his cup. "She was a shy woman. If I'd waited for her to say I love you, I might as well waited forever. But I'm of a notion anything come by too easy doesn't stand for much."

In the mirror over the back counter, I meet his eyes and read in them a look that says, *Is this happening to me? Is it my turn again? I never knew you got but one.*

So I don't say a word. I whip a rag around the top of a sugar container. I shine until the stainless steel glistens bright as the sunlight that lays out tiny dots on the tabletop next to the window, like a board set up for a game of Chinese checkers. At a corner table, Ernest Thomas and his brother, Ray, polish off the last of their grits and eggs. They take their leave then, each wearing a shirt with *Thomas Lumber Company* stitched across the back.

As I watch them, I think how to the outside world we probably don't stand for much, but in the Feed Room, we're real important to each other. We know the things to take note of, the things to overlook. I let Lucky steal food off the tables when nobody is around. Is it my fault she gets too brazen and tries to take if off people's plates? We don't ask Tan to leave when he sticks his case knife in the bottle of catsup—we change to packets.

I'm about to carry Ray and Ernest's dirty dishes into the kitchen when Merle pulls up out front. I stop with my hands still full and dart a glance toward Silo and Penny. They sit with their heads close together at the counter.

I get a tight, queasy feeling in my stomach as I watch Merle's hands ease the door of the pickup open with a groan. Her head pops into sight as big and round as a full moon, topped by a duckbill cap tilted to one side. She takes off the cap, runs her fingers through her hair. It's baby-thin and the wind tosses it about in ruffs that leave me staring at a pink scalp. She's heavyset with thick arms, but her scalp is as soft and delicate looking as an infant's. Slapping on her cap, she rocks it to and fro, anchoring it in place.

I strain forward and search for a glimpse, but don't see it. Still, I know it's there—the necklace with the half heart dangling in the valley beneath her plaid flannel shirt. The tight feeling in my stomach turns to the flutter of a hummingbird when Merle hitches up her jeans and slams the door to the pickup.

From here, Penny and Silo make me think of a closed unit, whispering together at the counter. Penny's face is slightly flushed. When she takes a breath, her chest goes up and down a little faster than usual.

Setting the dirty dishes on the counter, I straighten the napkins into a tidy pile. All of a sudden it's important that I keep them precision neat. One side of me wants to melt like a shadow into the wall, while the other wouldn't miss this for the world.

When I see Merle bend low at the window and shade her eyes to peep inside, my toes curl inside their crepe soles. Whether she's verifying what she already knows or just checking, I'm not sure. With her face to the glass, her eyes appear swimmy like she's peering from inside a goldfish bowl. When she spots Penny, she straightens, parts the door and steps over the threshold. Her moves are smooth as she crosses the room. She bounces lightly on the balls of her feet, her hips rolling easily, gliding like a well-oiled machine.

I'm studying her so hard, I jump when Sonny drops something in the kitchen. Then I hear running water. The sound, a curling noise, loops in and out like rain on a tin roof when it hits the bottom of the pot.

Silo faces the door. Penny has her back to it, so she hasn't seen Merle yet.

While Merle draws closer, I try to picture what she's seeing. A middle-aged man with a thunderous nose who fans out the last half-dozen hairs on the top of his head to deny he's balding. Nice dog curled at his feet, quiet, not bothering anybody.

When Silo glances up and sees Merle striding across the room, he follows her with his eyes, curious. He knows this has something to do with him, but can't figure out what.

Penny reads the new expression on his face and turns. When she sees Merle, she sits up straighter, pushes away from the counter—from Silo. I see her switch gears, the flame in her eyes lowered like somebody's closed a damper. She looks down at her hands and starts giving her cuticles a fierce workout.

Try as hard as I might, I can't take myself out of what's going on here. That's the thing about a small town. Stuff gets right in your face and stays there. For once, I can't figure out what I'm supposed to take note of, what I'm supposed to overlook. So I fail miserably at opening my mind to the possibility of what's coming next. Will Merle figure out what's going on between Penny and Silo or will Silo spot their necklaces first? It's a toss-up. So far, nobody's said a word. I stick a cup on the counter for Merle, fill it with coffee, top off Silo and Penny's, take what comfort I can from that.

As Merle nears the counter, her eyes glide past Silo like he's not there. When they lock on Lucky, they light up like she's won the lottery.

Amazed, I watch her bend down, scratch Lucky behind the ears.

"Hey, girl. What ya know? Pretty dog, pretty dog," she says, snapping her fingers.

I come from behind the counter to make sure Lucky hasn't been replaced by some dog I'm not familiar with. Sure enough, it's her. She's in a frenzy, trying to unwind from around the post while she wags her tail and licks Merle's face at the same time. Merle is on her knees now. She stretches her neck, twisting her chin back and forth to escape Lucky's feverish tongue. When she finally quiets down, Merle glances at Silo. "Blue tick?"

He nods.

"Don't think I've ever seen one with this coloring before. Brindle?"

He's about to answer when Merle leans over to examine the shading on Lucky's back. This is when the half-heart with the name *Penny* spelled across it drops from Merle's shirt and dangles like a neon sign.

I take a deep breath and hold it. Now my stomach is throwing a fit. I picture two ulcer germs, one stationed on each side chomping their way across to the center where they shake hands, congratulate themselves on winning the war.

Silo puts his coffee mug down so carefully you'd think it was fine china. Then he eases close for a better look. With his gaze fastened on the necklace, he blinks fast and snappy, checking to see if his eyes are in focus. When he's sure what he's seeing is what he's seeing, he cuts his eyes at Penny.

She fidgets on the stool, her head lowered. She watches him, but sneaks her glances from behind the curtain of hair draping her face. Their eyes dodge each other and the air between them fills with a silence thick as clam chowder.

Merle and Lucky are in the middle of the restaurant now, two kids romping and playing. Merle's cap flies off, lands behind a chair leg. She scrambles over to retrieve it with Lucky tugging at her shirtsleeve.

Silo sits still as a table lamp while he digests what he's seen. I imagine the pictures parading across his mind. When he finishes putting them together, it's his turn to pull away. I feel the fresh new life in him shrivel up. He closes into himself again, a peach wrapped tight around its pit.

I'm tempted to reach across the counter and take his hand, hold onto it to stop him from sinking back. *I wanted to tell you, Silo, I really did. But I couldn't. I'm sorry for that now. But don't go back. Anything is better than that.*

Then Penny lifts her head and looks straight at him. She runs the tip of her tongue across her bottom lip to moisten it. Her face breaks into a huge grin then. She chuckles softly and shakes her head. It's like she's saying, *Hey, Silo. I didn't mean to spring this on you but you were bound to find out sooner or later. So now what?*

I'm so busy watching Penny and Silo, I forget about Merle. When I notice her again, she's stopped roughhousing with Lucky. She leans back and rests on her heels, watching them, too.

Penny holds the grin longer than I could have. Silo doesn't give an inch. He holds her steady in his gaze and studies her like she's just sprouted a second head and he's curious about how she's managed such a thing.

By the time the grin finally drains from Penny's face, Merle catches on. Leaving Lucky to sit on her haunches and watch, Merle tucks in her shirttail and approaches the counter. The way she drapes an arm across Penny's shoulder, you'd think she'd just arrived and is tickled to be here. She nods at Silo, taking a sudden new interest in him.

For the first time, I feel like I need to jump in, so I come up with something really brilliant. "How about some coffee, Merle?" I slide her coffee cup toward her.

"Penny?" Merle raises an eyebrow.

Penny nods, the flush drained from her face along with the grin. "Maybe we just better go," she says.

"Whatever you say." Merle doesn't ask questions. She keeps her arm across Penny's shoulder while she eases off the stool. Silo watches them head for the door.

I stand behind the counter with the coffeepot poised over Merle's cup, mesmerized by the scene in front of me.

At the entrance, they stop and Merle glances back over her shoulder at Lucky. Lucky sits in the center of the room, watching them. When she sees that Merle is leaving, she gives a feeble whine and looks at Silo.

The dog is no favorite of mine, but I feel sorry for her. She's baffled by what's going on.

Then the three of them—Penny, Merle and Lucky—take turns looking at Silo. First Penny, then Merle. Now, it's Lucky's turn again. She figures this out and side-glances his way. Then she turns and trots across the room, her nails making a *click, click* sound on the polished tile. When she reaches Merle, she wags her tail and licks Merle's hand. Merle bends and pats Lucky on the head.

"Sit, pretty girl."

Lucky props on her haunches between Merle and Penny. Silhouetted in the doorway, the three of them face the counter, their gazes fixed on Silo.

Silo's mouth drops open. He can't believe what he's seeing. Neither can I. Finally, he closes his mouth and leans against the counter, his face drained.

Then, like she knows it's Silo's move but has decided to go out of turn, Merle whispers in Penny's ear.

Penny glances up in surprise. Merle nods.

In a nonchalant tone like she's asking him to pass the shaker so she can salt her fries, Penny says, "Coming, Silo?"

Even though I know full well the Feed Room is empty but for us—and thank God for that—I look around frantically for somebody to testify to this. For a second, I feel like dragging hungover Sonny out of the kitchen. But what's going on here doesn't need witnesses. It's between the three of them and Lucky. Still, I catch myself holding my breath.

I watch Silo struggle. I know he's trying to reconcile in his mind how some things in life stay true no matter how much we wish them otherwise. When he shifts on the stool and looks across the counter at me, I'm careful to keep a neutral face.

Then he slides off the leather seat and squares his shoulders and I know he's made up his mind. As he crosses the room, Lucky's wagging tail pounds up and down on the door behind her like she's beating on a drum. Merle moves to turn and open the door for them, but suddenly she stops and glances at Silo. He reaches around her and slides it open. Stepping back, he stands, fine and manly, while Merle and Penny and Lucky go out ahead of him. The door swishes closed behind them.

I'm not sure how Silo will fit into Penny and Merle's formula. Probably he doesn't either. Who was it said, miracles come in an instant, not when they're summoned, but of themselves—and to those who least expect them? I forget exactly how it goes, but I do know one thing. Silo thinks a man is judged by his convictions and he's always been true to his. That's not something that's likely to change.

Outside the wind picks up again. Mischievously, it catches a stray piece of paper and skips it past. I watch the paper dodge in and out, playing tag with the parking meters. Did the ground hog see his shadow today? I try to remember and can't. Samson will know.

Gathering up the dirty coffee mugs, I head for the kitchen so Sonny can stack them in the dishwasher. We'll need them for the lunch crowd, which will start pouring in any second now.

INTENTIONS

THIS MORNING WHEN I see Toy Man jog toward me on the trail, his feet pounding the concrete like a jackhammer, I know I'm later than usual. Ordinarily we meet on the first bend, rather than here where the curve is more wandering. Nothing moves above Toy Man's knees. His rigid body tilts from side to side like a robot. He's an old man, shrunken small, with a sparse gray beard lacing his chin and creases stenciled like birthmarks across his cheeks. I've learned to pamper my knees and judging from his knee braces, he probably wishes he had, too. Still, you have to admire his spunk. Every morning, he's out here pounding away in his rocking gait with its odd, contagious rhythm. Except for the beard and knee braces, he resembles my husband, Tinker.

Earlier, before the sun rose to this heat, a thick shade blanketed the path. Now the thin strips of sunlight slicing through the camphor trees feel surprisingly hot across my shoulders. Two men on bikes burst into the sunlight and swish past Toy Man.

"I know your take on fat people, but they're people, too," one of them says. "No shit," yells his buddy, then quickly ducks his head when he spots my gray hair.

I smile to let him know I've heard the word before. When Toy Man raises an index finger in greeting, I smile at him, too. Today my intention is to leave everybody who crosses my path feeling better. Lila, my counselor, says I have to start somewhere and that's somewhere.

Already this morning, I stopped to chat with Cello Lady from 205. She tells me she still pines for Elwood, her miniature dachshund with hair as silver as hers. For years, she practiced her music with Elwood curled at her feet. Of all the pieces she played, he liked Brahms best. Last fall, she had Elwood put to sleep. In the evenings now, I see her across the courtyard playing her cello alone.

I'm late this morning because *The Writer's Almanac* poem caught my attention. It had to do with kindness, and how, in order to know it, one must first know sorrow. Is this true? I ponder, trying to reconcile it with my intent, then stop. I'm told one of my problems is that I ponder too much. But before my mind clamps shut, an errant thought slips in. It's a fact that Cello Lady seems friendlier now that Elwood is gone.

I skirt a dead armadillo squashed flat into the pavement. A tire tread ribs the horny shell. I pause, wondering whether to pick it up and deposit it in a trashcan or let it lie. In this heat, it already emits a pungent, rotten smell. A can sits up ahead, but a good distance away. I picture myself with the armadillo slung over my shoulder, the odor permeating my shirt, the disgusting smell staying with me all day. Maybe I'll just scoot it to the edge of the trail. Then I remember how Lila says indecision is a sign of stress and decide to leave it where it lies. At the intersection up ahead, I'll loop back and retrace my tracks. If I change my mind, I can always pick it up on my way back.

Tinker turned seventy-six in June. Before he lost his mind, he used to say it's the intent that counts. Somehow it strengthens the resolve. I wonder how long my intent to leave a trail of smiles will last. In this week's session, Lila said one of my problems—and there are many, we're discovering—is that I walk around unconscious. "Oh, you're not the only one. Everybody does it. Sleepwalking, I call it. Stay in the present. Focus on what's in front of you." Since counselors are keen on eye contact, she holds firm to my gaze.

No, I want to explain, you don't understand. What's in front of me is the problem.

With Toy Man and the bikers out of sight, I check my minutes on my cell phone. It galls me to pay forty-five cents a minute over my plan. It isn't about the money; there's plenty of that. It's about being frugal and, of course, there's the not-paying-attention thing again. I don't mean being stingy like my daddy. Frugal is about waste; stingy is about being miserly. I picture Daddy at the kitchen table, content to rifle through his investment portfolio for hours. He liked to count his money but hated to spend it. One afternoon, he stopped his tallying and broke a molar cracking open a pecan for me with his teeth. He groaned and cupped his hand against his cheek as though if he didn't hold it tightly in place, the pain would spill out into his Procter & Gamble file.

Lila says we marry our daddies so they'll love us right this time, and then they disappoint us this time, too. By the time Tinker came along, I think I'd learned that love isn't about whether you do it right or wrong. Love is about love. The packaging it comes in is what's confusing. Love to Daddy meant cracking open pecans for you. To me, it meant bride dolls and red rubber boots and the whole set of Narnia books. Daddy was a child of the depression. How was he to know?

Tinker and I have had a good marriage. That's not to say it was all peace and quiet. I'm a strong believer in clearing the air—to a point, I've learned to add. A file resides on my desktop screen titled, *Keeping One's Mouth Shut Is Never Overrated*, and next to that is another labeled, *Opportunities I've Missed*.

"Do me a favor," he said once when I threw a head of cabbage across the room at him. "Next time, would you use lettuce? It's likely to do less damage."

"Tinker, the intent was to damage." Then we laughed. My throwing came to a halt, however, the day I threw a carving knife at him. I'd aimed to miss, but a knife is a knife anyway you look at it.

I have thirty minutes left on my phone, so I'm good. Sometimes I'm so close to my limit, I yearn to turn it off and pray nobody calls. I can't do it, of course. What if I'm needed? I hit the disconnect button too hard and the phone flips out of my hand into a hill of pampas grass. I watch, wishing I—not the phone— had disappeared into the bushes. Poof! Gone! Then no one will wonder, Where is she? Why isn't she here? Why can't we reach her?

Before I can head off the feelings, I'm lost, awash in shame and guilt. I try to live with no regrets, but of course, I don't. Who does? The intensity of trying to live like that, day in and day out, is daunting.

Bending, I retrieve the phone and glance up to see the General on his tricycle with the giant wheels—another testament to how we end up where we began. He's busy on his cell phone and raises his arm in a stiff salute. When sunlight breaks into a crazy polka-dot pattern across his face, I smile.

I've only recently begun walking the trail again. Immediately after it first opened, some fifteen years ago, I was here everyday. Before long, though, monotony drove me away. For a while, I tried T'ai Chi, and its languid to and fro had a gentle soothing effect, but walking is my thing. I love the briskness of it, my body moving with the efficiency and rhythm of a well-oiled machine.

Back then, a good portion of the trail was banked by stands of loblolly and palmetto thickets, while the rest was edged with solemn back yard fences. The fences were either boarded-up affairs used to seal the houses from sight or rickety chain lengths that closed in yards never intended for public view anyway. Now, I marvel at how the view has changed. Wildly blooming plumbago, the blossoms a too-beautiful-blue for a name that sounds like a back ailment, set off stately calla lilies that are backed by frivolous crape myrtles. The spruced-up look is a study in human nature. A backyard full of rusty lawn furniture and raggedy flowerbeds is okay for my family, but hold on! When anyone else is to see it, we'll take a second here and spiff it right up.

The day Tinker turned forty, he woke up and decided he was tired of being miserable. The next day, he filed for divorce from his first wife. That fall, he quit his job in criminal justice to begin teaching economics to college freshmen. He says men are reluctant to admit it, but one reason they divorce is because their wives get fat. Plus, he added, he and his brother had a knack for marrying women who felt entitled. Five years later, he and I were married. We were wed on a lovely day in April—a perfect day with the edges still cool and the middle balmy, not like today with heat that leaves perspiration dripping down my nose. I never remember to bring something to wipe with, so I use my shirttail now, leaving a wide swatch of damp. On the balmiest of days, I sweat. I do not glow—ever. I adore winter. I pile on coats, sweaters, fur-lined parkas, but once you're naked, you're done. There's no place else to go. In the mornings when I step outside for the newspaper, I long for a whisper of fall in the air. I haven't felt it yet, but every morning, I'm hopeful.

My husband Ed had been gone a year when Tinker appeared. I always make sure I say "gone" and not "I lost my husband," as if he was a missing earring or a set of car keys that I was likely to stumble on at any moment. He was gone, as in forever. For a long time, I said the words over and over, relearning the truth of them each time. That's what shock does to you.

Ed died in a freak accident on I-95. He slammed into a Toyota Camry whose driver had stopped to help another motorist change a tire. Two little girls in the Camry's back seat, three and four years old, were covered in blood. Miraculously, when the blood was cleaned away, they weren't hurt at all. The state trooper, who came to notify me, told me about the little girls. Knowing they'd survived helped. He didn't have to tell me whose blood they were covered in.

I still don't know which is worse, a sudden death like Ed's or a slow demise like the one I'm living through now with Tinker. The shock of one, the limbo of the other. Either way, it doesn't get easier.

I never knew about grief until Ed died, the weirdness of it, the pettiness. I found myself making the most bizarre statements. "I just attended the funeral of a dead person," I said to no one in particular, then had a sudden urge to laugh. When I finally removed my wedding ring, I felt as if suddenly everyone was staring at my empty ring finger. I hid the naked finger in my jeans pocket, covered it with my purse, sneaked it into the waistband of my skirt. I catch myself worrying my wedding band now and wonder if the finger can survive another wave of scrutiny.

Tinker said his only concern during his divorce was for his daughter Carlene, who was nineteen then. Old enough to know everything wasn't about her, but she usually didn't. And yet she still handled her parents split admirably. "Daddy, you don't have to explain a thing," she'd said. "What you and Mother do is your business."

Carlene calls Tinker and me the little people. She's a big-boned girl who leans toward heavy, like her mother. I fight that battle myself. Somehow I've managed to stay fairly slim, but it's a struggle. I'm not proud of the fact that in the weight war, you use the weapons at hand, but there it is. There's nothing like a fat ex-wife to keep you motivated.

My shoes make brisk thunks against the concrete. Despite my short legs, I walk fast. I move quickly past the tennis courts and bamboo thicket when suddenly I'm assailed by a whiff of tobacco smoke. When you quit, you develop a keen sense of smell. Suddenly alive and feisty, it perks up like an eager bloodhound. Glancing around, I spy a man behind a screened patio puffing away on a cigar. The pungent smoke floats through the mesh and hangs, contaminating the air. As ex-smokers feel it their right to do, I take a moment to gloat and feel superior. I then think of the things I steal from Walgreen's and my arrogance withers.

At the edge of the trail, a woman wearing gardening gloves burrows a hole in the soil with a trowel. She plops in a day lily, then fans herself. Behind her moss roses cascade from terra cotta pots on a tiered wrought-iron stand. This meticulous display of beauty is situated outside the fence. It's just for us. No one sees it but the joggers, the walkers, the bike riders who use the trail. The intent is to make our day a better one.

"How lovely. You must be a plant lover," I say and pause to admire her work. I understand her intent. It's one I'm convinced we share.

"Digging in the dirt is better than a Xanax," she says.

I meet two kinds of people on the trail. My trail friends, who are nameless until I give them a name. Our connections are the raised index fingers, the high fives, the salutes. I don't know if Toy Man has a wife waiting for him at home. I don't even know if he has a wife. Is the General really a general? I doubt. The other people, I know on a different level. They're neighbors, the checkout clerk at Publix, old friends, and colleagues.

Joe Sullivan, one of Tinker's friends, jogs toward me now in his bent-over arthritic gait. I wonder if he saw Verna Lassiter's obit in this morning's *Herald*. She taught with him and Tinker at the junior college. I wait to ask until he's close enough that I don't have to yell. He answers in his lifeless voice that was famous for lulling students to sleep. "No, but I'm not surprised." He bounces up and down on the balls of his feet. Every time we meet, I expect his voice to bounce, too, and am disappointed when it never does. "These days we don't catch colds and flu, we catch stuff that kills us. Cancer, heart failure, strokes." He throws up his hand and jogs off.

The question of how one catches cancer plays in my head. Our pharmacist at Colonial is almost even with me before I notice him. "How are you?" he asks, a greeting, not a question. "Putzing along," I say. Remembering I've forgotten to smile, I turn, but already he's moved quickly away. This is when I smile, fascinated by his rear end, each side jostling like a beach ball trying to get first in line.

In the beginning, I stole only flowers from the grounds of the condo complex, which, if you think about it, probably shouldn't even be considered a theft. I live in the complex. Didn't the flowers belong to me anyway? So my stealing started out innocently, I tell myself. I even had my reasons—reasons that Lila would label excuses. I can hear her now. One is about truth and the other about rationalizing. I know that; I'm no dummy. I also know stealing gardenias and jasmine isn't about battling our stale condo smells with fragrant blossoms any more than my stealing from Walgreens is about the stuff I steal. But say what you will about right or wrong, don't each of us make peace with what we do in our own way? The gardenia bushes were loaded this year. Who would miss the few I'd swiped?

Even after my stealing branched out to Walgreens, I kept my floral motif. Small boxes of Kleenex decorated in magnolia blossoms, ceramic picture frames with roses curling up the sides, freesia body wash. Gradually, the items I stole lost all sense of reason—PEZ candy dispensers, a compact with face powder and a mirror, Scotch tape sticky on both sides. I secrete the articles in my shoulder bag, feeling like a teenager who's out to spite her divorcing parents rather than a sixty-five-year-old woman who takes pride in how, over the past ten years, she's successfully divested herself of stuff. I discovered that you spend the first fifty years of your life accumulating things and the second fifty ridding yourself of what you've accumulated. Then, just when I started traveling light, I began stealing things. But like I said, I don't delude myself that the stealing is about stuff. Since there's no logic, I try not to think about the why or what will happen if I'm caught. I just do it. My guest room looks like a supply warehouse, with boxes of plastic pushpins stacked beside cans of marked-down tuna and economy sized packages of Barney toothbrushes.

The selection is best at Walmart even though, according to Carlene, I'm not supposed to shop there. She is passionate about their low wages, their unfair policies toward women. For my own principles, I'm willing to be inconvenienced just so much and then I say to heck with it. I make sure the recyclables wind up in the recycle bin; I use stick deodorant rather than aerosol spray, but that's about it. Carlene drives a Prius. She uses a mesh string bag for groceries. She marches for pro-choice and volunteers for Planned Parenthood. She takes her principles so seriously, it seems only right that I should, too. What can I say? That Walmart has the best plant selection in town doesn't seem a good enough argument. So I sneak into their superstore for the orchids that adorn our coffee table. I pay for the orchids but can't resist stealing a bottle of Bayer while I'm there.

Although Tinker's mother had wanted him to be an attorney like his dad, Tinker started out wanting to be a mortician of all things. He worked at Dunwitty's Funeral Home in high school and loved it. In those days, hearses served the dual purpose of ambulances, too. When he realized that what he loved wasn't embalming dead people, but driving the ambulances fast, he joined the state patrol after college. Finally he wound up teaching driver's education at a federal training center in Jacksonville. "Reckless drivers are killers," he explained when we met, "especially when they drive fast, too. The idea is to drive cars fast when it's necessary, but learn to do it safely."

After such a promising start, he was shocked at forty to find himself no longer driving cars fast, but stuck behind an administration desk with a wife at home who thought she was better than everybody else.

Personally, I didn't see how you could drive fast and safe at the same time. I thought it was either/or, but somehow in Tinker's mind, the reasoning made sense. For all of his love of speed, he was the most cautious driver I knew—before I had to take away his car keys.

I don't tell Lila about the stealing. What would she think? I'm no thief. Then I'm hit by the incongruity of the thought, like using *fast* and *safe* or *steal* and *innocent* in the same breath.

Behind me, I hear voices. I glance over my shoulder to see three runners approach, young men jogging three abreast across the trail. They close ranks to pass and I hear one of them say a little breathlessly, "When she wants a heart to heart and you sit down for an eye to eye, you say nothing."

"Nothing?" the middle runner asks.

"Nothing!"

When they spot me grinning, one of them yells, "Isn't that right? You don't want us to solve your problems. Just listen, right?"

"It's all in the book," I shout as they speed past. "Read the book! *Men are from Mars, Women Are from Venus.*"

As I yell out the title, I realize they've probably never heard of it. The book came out years ago. Tinker and I loved it. It put into words so much of what we already knew. Men's thought patterns are direct and linear—the facts ma'am, just the facts—while women's thoughts are more detailed and rounded, stuffed with sidebars and vivid colors.

"Oh, Daddy, what do you know?" Carlene scoffed when he dropped one of the book's pearls into a conversation. I had to wonder what made her think she knew so much; she'd never even had a serious relationship. But like any good lawyer, she tends to think she knows everything about everything. Then I chide myself. That's not true. Sometimes she's wrong. She knows it, but never admits it. She still argues then; she just argues less.

Green Running Shorts whips around the bend now, the one where I usually meet Toy Man. She's a regular, but someone who looks away at the last second before making eye contact. I don't intrude, just glance away, too. When she dodges my eyes, I know it's nothing personal. It's about keeping her space private and demanding respect. It's the same reason we stare at the ceiling while we ride in an elevator. It's why, in community living where we live one on top of the other, we keep a cautious distance from our neighbors—friendly but detached.

Tinker never got it that everybody in the complex wasn't his new best friend. Never in his entire life had he had to remind himself to smile.

At the intersection, I wheel and head back down the trail. When I reach the trashcan, I see that someone has put the crushed armadillo in a cardboard box and placed the box beside the can. It sits now, tidy and snug, awaiting the next pick up. I chuckle to myself. Tinker used to say, don't just do something, stand there.

When I hear the scream of a fire truck ahead of me, I glance up as it whips onto Mauphas. Automatically, I pick up speed. I take the shortcut behind the tennis courts. I stumble into a jog. Did he turn on a burner and forget? Did he find the matches? I break into a run, leaping over curbs and drainage ditches. Then it dawns on me and I pull myself up short. I don't need to hurry. What's my rush?

I lean over with my hands on my thighs and catch my breath. I let my hands drop and dangle loosely in front of me. Staying bent, I watch them swing back and forth. Again I remind myself: I have all the time in the world. I remind myself that he's safe, he's well-cared for, he's happy—the litany I tell myself that lets me put my head down on my pillow and sleep at night.

Carlene thought he needed to be put away. "He's not my daddy anymore. Daddy's gone. Besides, didn't he always say, as long as I'm in my right mind, don't put me into one of those places, but if I lose my mind, then whatever?"

I never heard Tinker say that. Where was I? Sleepwalking again? But by this time, I'd run out of arguments. Besides, I was never a match for Carlene.

I straighten and take a deep breath, the humidity hitting my face like a wet rag. Turning back toward the corner crosswalk, I ignore the throbbing in my temple. I focus on what's in front of me. A kid in a blue convertible with the top down stops and gives me the go ahead. I wave him on. The beat in my forehead ebbs, then stills. The key to crossing in traffic is to take an immovable stance. I've learned that no matter how much the man in the tan Taurus yearns to prove he's a gentleman, I stand firm.

A silver Subaru stops on one street corner and an SUV glides to a halt on the other. I lift my arm to signal that I'm about to cross. I step off the curb, confident that I have the right of way.

Suddenly, from the corner of my eye, I see a bicycle speeding toward me. The cyclist sweeps up to the corner. Hesitating, he glances at me and both cars. "I don't understand what's going on here," he announces impatiently and barrels forward, wheeling around the corner so close I jump back. My toe catches and I teeter. When I've righted myself, I explode. "You idiot! Are you blind? Can't you see I'm about to cross!" I know the jerk has heard me. He can't help but hear me because I'm screaming like a banshee.

He doesn't look back, just pedals faster. I'm left with nothing but my rage and his receding back in its neon yellow racing shirt. I stare at his tight, hard arms, the pump of his sinewy calves. Like a wild animal, I want to claw at his flesh, I want to tear the muscles from his taut limbs.

Finally, sunlight, tears and sweat meld him and his racing bike into a blur. "You despicable insect," I mutter, a parting shot that's ineffectual and futile. I drag myself back onto the curb.

Spent now, done in by my fury, I can only follow him with my eyes. As he swerves around the corner, he is outlined against the sky like the piece to a jigsaw puzzle. Then he disappears, swallowed by the distance. For the longest time I stand and stare at the empty patch of blue he's left behind.

JACOB'S LADDER

YANCY PLAYS A game with himself as he watches his six-year-old niece weave back and forth on the concrete wall that separates his yard from his brother Zack's. In the game, Yancy pretends that if Mary Ellen topples off on Zack's side of the wall, his brother has to take care of her for the rest of her life. Yancy thinks playing the game is probably the worst thing he's ever done. He thought he was made of better stuff than this, yet he's played the game for the past six weeks since their sister Lily died.

So far Mary Ellen has wound up on his side of the wall every time.

As the chubby little girl struggles for a foothold, the shiny red hair bow caught atop her head bobs up and down. Mary Ellen loves red—red hair bows, red lollipops, red sandals, red fire engines. Before Lily died, Mary Ellen practically lived on the red swing set beside the rain tree, swinging for hours with Cherrie, Yancy's three-year-old. Now Mary Ellen ignores the swing set and makes a beeline for the concrete wall. The wall separates his yard from Zack's on the right and their neighbor Mr. Gleason's on the left and the lake in back. Because of the children, Yancy keeps a double lock on the gate to the lake.

After the funeral, Yancy and his wife Rita took the little moon-faced girl with the sleepy eyes home with them. It seemed the natural thing to do since she loved playing with Cherrie. As Rita had pointed out to Yancy and Yancy had pointed out to Zack, the set up was only temporary—until something permanent could be arranged

Zack steps out of his screened door onto the back porch. Clutched in his hand is a brown paper sack full of boiled peanuts. Plucking a peanut from the bag, he opens it with his teeth. He nods at Yancy, eyes Mary Ellen, then quickly looks away. Yancy knows how his brother thinks. To acknowledge the child's presence means he has to deal with her. He's not ready for that. In fact, Yancy was flummoxed this morning when Zack brought up the subject over their early coffee at the NicNac Grill. Picking nervously at a shaving nick on his chin, he said, "I don't think Charlene could raise another child. Our own two about did her in."

Charlene must be pressuring Zack. Yancy couldn't see his brother broaching the subject otherwise. What Zack said was true. His wife had never been around children before she and Zack married, so the only thing she knew to do when hers cried was cry along with them. Even now, with both of the children grown and out on their own, she's forever running to the doctor with a nervous stomach.

"I remember how frazzled Charlene stayed when Ben and Gail were little," Yancy said. He left hanging in the air between them, *What about my wife? Isn't she to be considered?*

But then, they both knew the question with Rita wasn't if she *could* handle another child; it was if she *would*.

Yancy shades his eyes with his hand and squints up at the sky. Popcorn clouds laze overhead. Rain is in the forecast. They need it. The long dry spell has left the St. Augustine grass a dingy green. In the distance, a thundercloud looms.

Mary Ellen teeters and Zack stands motionless with a peanut halfway to his mouth. When she reaches the post and regains her footing, he pops the peanut into his mouth. Then he removes his glasses and wipes his sweaty forehead with his shirtsleeve. In the sunlight, his eyes shine a startling blue, like a car fender recently waxed.

Across the concrete wall on the left, Mr. Gleason watches Mary Ellen, too, the chisel in his hand poised above the snout of the blue tick hound he's carving in the tree stump. The stump, maybe twelve feet around, is from an ancient live oak that was lost in the recent hurricane. About three feet up from the ground, the trunk divides and rises another three feet into the air like a "V." Mr. Gleason said the hurricane did him a favor by taking out the tree. For years he'd talked about the wood sculpture he would carve when he retired from the city. The two blue ticks he'd sculpt on one arm of the trunk; on the other would be two Boston bulls.

Yancy is surprised at the happy plaid suspenders Mr. Gleason wears to hold up his denim shorts. *Happy* isn't a word Yancy ordinarily associates with the man. Years ago, he had a lot to say—all of it bad—when Yancy's daddy divorced his mother and married Carol Skywalker, the new financial officer at 2nd National. Mr. Gleason believes men should be held accountable. Ordinarily, Yancy finds this an admirable trait, but Mr. Gleason's version is rigid and inflexible. It's more about judgment than accountability and leaves him looking down on people.

Mr. Gleason keeps his eyes peeled on the little girl. When he sees that she's safely balanced again, he shoots Yancy a look, one that makes Yancy feel as if the old man is reading his thoughts. Given his thoughts of late, that makes Yancy squirm. He can't believe the fix he's in. He fights a sudden urge to yell, to pound his fist on something hard, anything to escape this trapped feeling. He knows lashing out won't help. What will? What would he wish for if he could? That he didn't have to play the game; that Zack would take Mary Ellen without a fuss, that Lily was not dead, that she was back with them sporting a new liver that worked, a fresh one they'd taken out of someone else and given to her on the Discovery Channel. They do it all of the time.

Yancy listens to the slide of Mr. Gleason's chisel. The old man is using the slick side now. It whispers against the wood, caressing and polishing as it carves. His goal, he says, is to finish his tree art using the chisel, a chain saw and a grinder. Mr. Gleason has tried working with only a saw and grinder but can't maneuver in the close places without the chisel—the neck, around the eyes, the slender tails. The dogs with their secret nooks and crannies require more precision than the saw and grinder give him.

When their dad left, everybody's attitude toward their father changed, including Mr. Gleason's. Yancy didn't expect that. In fact, he wrestled with how, for some people, his father's one despicable act cancelled out every decent thing he'd ever done before. Yancy can't help wondering about the side of human beings that calculates lives like this. He wonders about the same quality in himself.

Yancy loves his father, not like before he left when he could do no wrong, but in some distant way that has little to do with either of them—except on those days when Yancy feels overwhelmed and needs someone to blame. The idea that his dad is judged by a single act doesn't seem fair. But then, life isn't fair. If it were, he wouldn't have left in the first place.

Holding the chisel at a certain angle, Mr. Gleason makes delicate little riffs in the wood. Ruffles of soft fur emerge. He says he follows two simple rules: make small cuts and know when to stop. As he bends eye-level to scrutinize the dog's chin, his belly, once taut and flat, laps over his belt buckle. In his mind's eye, Yancy pictures the old man with a rotting liver, his skin a rancid yellow, his stomach swollen and filled with the fluid that will eventually drown him.

The absurdity of his thinking staggers Yancy. He wishes he lived two thousand miles away in a cabin on a creek bank with nobody to read his thoughts. As foolish and outrageous as his wishes seem, he's careful they don't involve Mary Ellen. The game he plays fools with her fate enough as it is.

It wasn't her fault Lily had pulled her around in the little red wagon until Mary Ellen was four and finally learned to walk. It wasn't her fault that Lily had rocked the child to sleep every night of her life. Now with her mother gone, Mary Ellen scarcely sleeps at all. She's wide awake even when Yancy and Rita take turns rocking her until their arms feel paralyzed. No matter how much they rock or how gently they lay her down beside Cherrie in the trundle bed the two of them share, Mary Ellen stares up at them in the darkness. Then she cradles her arms across her chest and rocks back and forth. Yancy worries that she'll wander in the dark while they're sleeping. So far, she's simply hugged herself until dawn.

On the wall, Mary Ellen stops for a second and cocks her head to one side as if she's listening for a far-off sound. Then she flails her arms, her hands batting at a horsefly circling her head.

"She's going to fall again, " Mr. Gleason says.

Yancy dodges the old man's eyes. *Why don't you say what you mean?* he wants to yell back. *What you're really saying is, What's wrong with you boys? Are you blind? Can't you see what's about to happen? Or is it that you don't want to see, that you don't care?*

Instead, Yancy busies himself examining a clod of dirt stuck to his shoe heel. A shroud of shame, so heavy his arms ache, closes over him. He scrapes his sole against the top step until he worries the dirt loose. The clump falls off without breaking, a perfect little one-inch cast of his shoe tread. He feels like sailing over the wall and lifting Mr. Gleason by his shirt collar. *It's easy for you. You don't have to deal with what you see. You aren't the one held accountable.*

Mary Ellen throws out her arms, then curls them in against her chest, trying to corral the pesky fly. She moves sluggishly, as if she's treading water. Like everything she does, it's a struggle— except when she has a crayon in her hand. Then something magical happens. The clumsy little girl vanishes. Her fingers are fine and sure. Her drawings are bold. They come alive bursting with color. She draws dancing bears, acorns, scarlet dragons, seesaws, daffodils, bumblebees and masses of red birds that fly off the page.

Mr. Gleason moves his hand along the wood, feeling the bridge of the snout for rough spots. He uses elbow grease and tungsten oil rubbed into the wood to bring out the sheen. He reminds Yancy it's the finish that counts. It has to be perfect.

Yesterday when Mary Ellen toppled from the wall, she'd shut her pink-rimmed eyes as tight as fists and shrieked. With the tail of his shirt, Yancy wiped away her tears. "Come along," he said, the way he'd learned to talk to her to make her hush. "I'll show you how to build a Jacob's Ladder."

Mary Ellen's cries stopped, turned off like a spigot. "What's a Jacob's Ladder?"

Yancy flicked away a blade of grass glued to her chin. "I'll show you."

"How'd you do that?"

"How'd I do what?"

"Build a Jacob's Ladder?"

"I didn't yet."

"Oh."

Rita stood at the sink in the kitchen, peeling apples for a pie. Cherrie played with her Easy Bake beside the real stove, her hands caked in cookie dough. At the sound of the back door, they both looked up. When Rita saw them, she shook her head.

"Don't start, " Yancy warned.

Rita cocked an eyebrow. "Who me?"

Yancy pulled a chair from the table and lifted Mary Ellen into it. She gazed at him with her thumb in her mouth and her arms akimbo on the tabletop while he searched in a kitchen drawer for the string. With Rita watching and Cherrie looking on wide-eyed, Yancy tied a knot in the string and looped it over his index finger. He'd spun it back and forth and flipped it across his wrist once when Rita asked, "Yancy, what on earth are you doing?"

"Building a Jacob's Ladder."

"A what?"

He'd looped each thumb twice when Rita said, "If you're looking for something to do, why don't you teach her to tie her shoes?"

The string slipped past Yancy's little finger and caught on his wrist.

"Stuff it, Rita," he said and balled his hands into fists, leaving the string dangling.

Mary Ellen took her thumb from her mouth and held it out in front of her like a lollipop. "Is that a Jacob's Ladder?"

"Not yet."

Satisfied with his answer, she popped her thumb back into her mouth.

Yancy stared at the knotted string. *When did Rita and I begin speaking like this to each other?* he wondered. *I love my wife; she beguiles me. She always has.* She could be difficult, he knew, but he could still lose himself in the intoxicating smell of her, in her luscious hair, in the richness of her skin against his lips. She hasn't said Mary Ellen can't stay with them permanently, but the creases around her lips have deepened and she's become silent and efficient. She changes the toilet paper before the roll is empty and straightens over and over again the dishtowels on the sink. The night before, she'd woken Yancy grinding her teeth in her sleep. She's forever telling him his take on life is too simplistic. *Life isn't fair.* He says the words, but in truth he doesn't believe it.

But she's wrong about that. What he doesn't believe is that he should stop hoping that life will be, that he should stop doing his part to make it fair.

Rita studied the apple in her hand, avoiding his eyes. Even after her sarcastic remark, he couldn't help thinking how lovely she was, how translucent her skin, how gracefully she moved. When she came into his life, everything else became a blur.

For a moment she chewed on her bottom lip. Then she made a funny face at Mary Ellen and the child giggled. Gently, Rita pulled Mary Ellen's thumb from her mouth. "Honey, don't do that. You're too big to suck your thumb." She slipped a slice of the apple between Mary Ellen's fingers.

With a cry, Cherrie jumped up from her toy oven and snatched the apple from Mary Ellen's hand. For a second Mary Ellen stared at her, then she giggled again.

"Cherrie!" Rita and Yancy yelled together.

"Give that back to her. You know better than that," Rita said. "Here's a piece for you."

Mary Ellen's giggles turned into bursts of laughter. She loved them all. She always had. And she never doubted that they loved her—even when they didn't act as if they did.

When Mary Ellen lifted her arms, Rita dropped to her knees and hugged the child. "Oh honey, you are so sweet," she said. Glancing at Yancy, she rose hurriedly and gathered the peels from the counter. She plopped them into the sink and flipped the switch on the disposal. A grinding roar filled the room as the disposal chewed and spit. Yancy had meant to replace the broken part.

"He could take her at least part of the time," Rita said over the racket.

"I'm working on it."

"You're afraid to ask him."

"I am not!"

"Then what is it?"

At that moment, she switched off the disposal.

"It's not that!" he shouted, his words splintering the sudden quiet.

Yancy hears a low rumble of thunder in the west. On the wall, Mary Ellen's lips are pressed together and her eyes are fixed on the corner post nearest the street. She walks only on the wall between his house and Zack's. She never ventures to the section that faces the lake or Mr. Gleason's side of the yard. As far as she's concerned, neither the old man nor his tree art exists.

Zack tosses a peanut shell across the yard, trying to skip it like a pebble over water but it goes no place. Mr. Gleason's chisel makes a crunching sound against the wood. He's absorbed in his work now. The armpits of his blue chambray shirt are ringed with sweat. Oak is hard wood; carving it is hard work. He's forever replacing chisels. When he stands to catch his breath, his shape is etched like a chess piece against the dark clouds gathered behind him. Mr. Gleason wasn't born knowing how to carve a blue tick out of a tree trunk, but under the ministering of his chisel, the tree trunk emerges into something wondrous. This wondrous beauty, like Mary Ellen's paintings, is filled with hopeful promise.

Zack swears redemption of the soul comes only through Jesus Christ. Yancy doesn't know about that, doesn't even know if he has a soul—thoughts he'd never say aloud to anyone he knows. If he does have a soul and if it needs redeeming, its salvation, he believes, will come from deeds like Mr. Gleason's tree art or the colors like sunshine in Mary Ellen's drawings. Beautiful deeds done with loving hands kindle in Yancy a feeling he thinks of as divine.

Mr. Gleason revs up the grinder. The roaring motor jars Yancy back into the moment. It sounds like his disposal—only worse. Mary Ellen ignores the noise and moves her hands in slow measured patterns of bends and curves. For a second Yancy thinks she's honing in on the fly again. Then he glances up to see an ibis perched close by. He watches the child's fingers outline the sleek shape of the bird's bill dipping into a curved point at the end. She works in a logical fashion, breaking it down into steps that make sense even to Yancy. Suddenly he feels the magic in her fingertips. He understands, as he won't a moment later, what makes her drawings extraordinary. Everyone has a reason for being. Everyone.

With the image of the ibis buried in her fingers, Mary Ellen kneels and touches the day lily blooming beside the low wall. She's stacked a pile of bricks against the wall and uses them as steps. Each time she reaches the top, she looks around astonished, as if she's wound up there purely by accident. She turns her hand, fascinated by the pollen the day lily has left on her fingertips.

Dropping her hand, she takes a step. Her trek is methodical and repetitious. When she reaches the corner post, she pauses and separates the philodendron leaves that block her view. She peers solemnly up and down Lester Road. Turning, she picks her way to the post at the opposite end and stands staring toward the lake. When wind from the approaching storm ruffles the water in choppy waves, she claps her hands, applauding the wind for its fine performance.

The concrete wall and flowers pop up everywhere in her drawings. The wall struts down the center of the page with the lake stationed like a mirror at one end. Blossoms rim the edges of the page. The wandering rose bush lacing the wall twines across the page and holds the colors on the paper.

Zack eats the last boiled peanut and crumples the empty bag in his hand. "You're going to fall and break your neck," he yells.

That's a switch, Yancy thinks. Zack might not be ready to do anything about her yet, but at least he's acknowledging that she exists.

Both he and Yancy know she'll fall. She always does; it's only a matter of when. There is a roundness about her when she hits the ground. She thumps like a plump melon. Their saving grace is that the wall is low-standing, four feet high at the most, so it's not likely she'll be injured—at least this is what Yancy tells himself. He cautions her not to climb the wall, but doesn't stop her when she does.

The thundercloud is overhead now. A sprinkle of rain begins and she lifts her face to let the mist bathe her cheeks. Startled by a smart clap of thunder that explodes nearby, she screams. Stepping wildly, she tries for a foothold but her foot slips.

Yancy automatically reaches out, but of course, from his back porch where he stands, he's too far away to catch her. She lands in a dip in the lawn that will be a mud puddle soon if the rain keeps up. More than once, Zack has filled the sunken area with sod to even the ground on his side of the wall.

Yancy steps back onto his porch. "Well, I guess that settles it," he says. He turns to go inside as if he and Zack have made up the game together and both of them know the rules. Yancy doesn't stop to think about the words he's just spoken. Only later, when the game and Rita's leaving are things of the past, when the weather-beaten dog sculptures sit like great frozen sphinxes in Mr. Gleason's backyard, does Yancy remember that Zack never said a word.

With his hand on the doorknob, Yancy hesitates. Even though he knows Mr. Gleason is watching and wills himself to keep his eyes in front of him, he can't help glancing across at the old man. Sure enough, he leans against the tree trunk, his thumbs in his suspenders, watching. Grudgingly, Yancy turns his gaze toward his brother.

Zack stands over Mary Ellen, looking down. Yancy imagines the child peering up with frightened eyes, yet Zack doesn't move. Why doesn't he pick her up? What is he thinking? From his stance, Yancy swears his brother could be searching for a handle to pick her up by. When he doesn't find one, he turns toward Yancy.

Across the wide stretch of yard, their eyes lock. Yancy releases the doorknob and eases slowly to the edge of the porch. Suddenly he understands what he hasn't before. Zack, who's never been afraid of anything, is afraid of Mary Ellen. The pleading look in his eyes is pitiful. *Don't make me do this. I can't do this.*

Yancy turns and gazes down the wide stretch of lawn toward the lake, past the shedding rain tree, the ground beneath it a solid carpet of gold. A break in the wind has left the face of the lake smooth, like the mirror in Mary Ellen's drawings. A sound begins deep in his throat. When it threatens to become a moan, he cuts it off short. Zack's fear isn't that Mary Ellen is hurt. He knows she's not; she's fallen before. His fear is of touching her, of feeling her chubby arms encircle his neck. He's afraid of the pools of emptiness in her unblinking eyes.

Yancy wishes he didn't feel sorry for his brother, but he does. What we have the power to do, someone said, we have the power not to do. He doesn't believe this. He knows Zack can't control how he feels about Mary Ellen anymore than Yancy can control his own jumbled feelings about what he sees now. His thoughts, yes, but his emotions, they're a different story. He's surprised to find mingled with his pity for Zack is a strange sense of power over him, too. For once, Yancy has the edge on his brother. He savors the feeling, lets it wash over him. Wrapped up in it is a lifetime of being afraid to say what needs to be said, of living with the permanent knot in his stomach that peace at any cost plants there.

Yancy is so lost in his thoughts that he's completely forgotten Mary Ellen. When he thinks of her now, the moan deep in his throat thickens. Then he also remembers the game and his sudden surge of power disappears.

Years ago Zack had said Mary Ellen was Lily's punishment for falling in love with a son-of-a-bitch who wasn't suitable husband material. Yancy was appalled. *What's that you're always saying, Zack? From your lips to God's ears.* In fact, when Zack had made his sanctimonious remark, Yancy couldn't think of anything that bad he'd ever done. Now he can. That game. That stupid game!

The rain has picked up. Fat drops spatter his face and shirt. He crosses the yard and is there to catch Mary Ellen when Zack lifts her and swings her feet-first over the wall. She drops into Yancy's arms, rubbing tears from her eyes with the back of her hands.

Zack brushes at the rusty stains the pollen has left on his sleeve.

"Don't worry, Zack, what she has isn't contagious," Yancy says. Zack flinches and drops his hand.

Yancy hears the surliness in his words. Once he'd have been shocked at how mean-spirited he's become. His first mean thought was the hardest to live with, the next one came easier, and the next even easier. Now they parade unchecked through his mind.

For a second, Zack seems lost for words. Then he says, "It's not that simple."

"No, you're right, it's not."

"You'll make a Jacob's Ladder now?" Mary Ellen whispers.

A billowing gust of wind sweeps across the yard, stirring the cloud of winter-white snow hair against her cheek. Yancy rights the lopsided red bow and pushes back the thin strands of hair. Cupping her face in his hand, he thinks of how the colors in her drawings tease the eye. Their fire burns hot enough to scorch the fingertips.

"Not until you've learned to tie your shoes," he says.

He looks up at the sky. If he races, they'll just make it to the shelter of the porch before the real downpour begins. From the corner of his eye, he sees Mr. Gleason watching them.

Just make sure you notice which of us is the accountable one, Yancy thinks.

With Mary Ellen cradled in his arms, he bends and shields her from the rising wind and rain. Only when he stumbles up onto his back stoop does it hit him. He can be as mean-spirited and despicable as he likes, but nothing can change the fact that now Mary Ellen belongs to him. He's saddled with her forever.

Suddenly, he feels himself exploding. It's not fair. It's just not fair. The weight of his anger drags down on his arms, his legs. They're so heavy. He can't lift them; they're impossible to lift. The child slips, her cheek scraping the doorsill as she slides from his arms. Mr. Gleason has rushed up on his back step to escape the rain, but he still watches as Mary Ellen slips to the floor.

Yancy turns to find Rita staring at him, too. He could be performing onstage in a play. The play is in its closing scene, a scene his wife watches from the kitchen window. What happens now? Will Rita leave him? A tremor shakes him, fear radiating through his exhausted body. He can't bear to think of her leaving.

Meanwhile, Mary Ellen hasn't made a sound. She shivers, chilled from the rain. Wrapping her arms across her chest, she rocks back and forth, hugging herself as her gaze flickers between Rita and Yancy.

Yancy is so weary, he feels buried beneath the exhaustion. When he picks up Mary Ellen, her pale face floats before him. He'll give her supper and a bath. Then he'll put her to bed and fall into bed himself. When he passes the kitchen window, he glances up. Mr. Gleason's wood sculptures are poised like great hulking shadows against the stark concrete wall.

Tomorrow when I'm thinking clearly, Yancy says to himself, when I'm not so drained, tomorrow I'll figure things out.

WIND CHIMES

THE RACKET AT the end of the driveway sounded as if it came from a rock band rather than the two dim shadows outlined in the gray-tinged dawn. Milky streaks of morning threaded the silver maples that edged the lawn, and the shadows emerged slowly as women. One was stout and middle-aged with gray hair caught in a thick braid that fell halfway down her back. The second was younger, but heavy, too, in jeans and what looked like a long-sleeved blouse buttoned at the neck. Both of the women held placards the size of stop signs above their heads. With her free hand, the younger woman, the one making the noise, beat a tambourine ferociously against her thigh. I squinted to read what was on her sign and felt my stomach lurch when I saw the words: Baby Killer.

Focusing on a fox squirrel that scampered outside of the kitchen window rather than the scene on the driveway, I tried to still my anxious insides. I watched Lucy from the corner of my eye as she surveyed the commotion outside her house. How did it feel to be called a baby killer? I couldn't imagine. Since I hailed from a part of the country that believed an abortion was about killing, I'd heard the words for as long as I could remember. I'd just never heard them aimed at anybody I knew. We didn't let the fact that we thought abortions were wrong stop us from having them, but it did stop us from talking about them.

61

"I don't believe in abortions," my father had said at the clinic in Savannah where he took my sister for her first one. "But my Sadie. . ." he'd finished, sliding the stack of crumpled bills across the counter. Then he'd come to sit beside Sadie and me in the waiting room, leaving the receptionist to fill in the blanks. Somehow he'd convinced himself he could have it both ways.

When I had awakened that morning, Lucy was already in the kitchen, the coffee made and cinnamon oatmeal bubbling softly. She'd heard me behind her and turned, running her fingers through her short black hair, then tucking it behind each ear. Even at that early hour, each ear lobe was garnished in an elegant gold loop. She'd once studied ballet, so I knew beneath her loose caftan was the lithe body of a dancer.

Lucy had just poured us two steaming cups of coffee when the jarring beat of the tambourine shattered the early morning quiet, washing over us like an ocean of sound.

"Oh my goodness, what's that awful noise?" I'd exclaimed, moving to the window.

Lucy had merely put a finger to her lips shushing me as if I were the one making the racket. "I just hope they don't wake Logan and Jim," she'd said.

I waited for her to go on. When she didn't, the two of us stood in silence and watched the raw scene outside. I couldn't know what Lucy was thinking, but knew if I were in her shoes I'd be frantically petitioning the Protest Gods. *Please, name your price. Whatever I have to sacrifice, take it! Make them go away! Just for today, while our guests are here.*

"I'm in Toledo on Monday doing procedures, on Tuesday I'm in Detroit, in Savannah on Wednesday, and on Friday, I'm in Jacksonville," Lucy's husband Logan had said last night at dinner, just after Jim and I arrived.

"I carry a weapon, too, and it's not for hunting. Romeo and Prince are retired now." He'd nodded toward the two spotted pointers lying outside on the patio.

I'd been struck by how Logan didn't say *gun*; he'd said *weapon*, an ominous word for a man so drenched in good will. He was an Irish leprechaun virtually gushing with best wishes for his friend Jim, who had finally found himself a bride. Actually, Jim had found himself a bride about three years before, but the two of us were just now visiting Lucy and Logan for the first time.

While Lucy had busied herself setting out plates of capers, chopped parsley and roasted red peppers, I'd sat across from the men on the couch, separated in an odd way from Logan's animation and effusiveness. In fact, I began to feel ignored and invisible, as if my spot on the couch was a mere blank space.

Finally, as if I'd suddenly popped back into the void, Logan has turned to me and smiled. "And a welcome to you. A fine welcome to you."

And before I could stop myself, I was beaming, too.

"Last week Logan backed the car into one of them," Lucy said, still standing before the window.

When I looked up in alarm, she went on quickly, "It was an accident, of course. He didn't see her in his rearview mirror and only tapped her, so she wasn't hurt. If they put one toe on our property, it's trespassing. The woman he hit was a new one, fairly young, who didn't know the rules about where to stand."

The women outside turned to watch a convertible with its top down creep to a stop behind them. A man about my age, early fifties, with silver hair that was tousled and boyishly unkempt, slid from behind the wheel. Considering his Humpty Dumpty body, I was surprised at how quickly he'd climbed from the car. With a smooth efficiency, he lifted an enormous saxophone from the back seat. When he raised the instrument to his lips and moistened the mouthpiece, the tambourine stilled. The women stepped back and he took over the music. On the fourth note, I recognized the song he was playing. "Amazing Grace."

On the drive up, Jim had explained how Logan had practiced obstetrics and gynecology for many years in this small Midwestern town where, even today, the milkman delivered milk through the back door and set the bottles directly onto the bottom shelf of the fridge. But after a simple delivery that went horribly wrong, where both the mother and baby had died and a lengthy lawsuit followed, Logan gave up private practice and took a job with Planned Parenthood.

Our visit with them was part of Jim's apology for yelling, "I know it's your hair, but I have a right to say what you do with it." I'd "shorn" my locks—his words, not mine—without his permission.

Although to some, this might have seemed a small thing, when he said it to me, I'd thought the top of my head would explode. Once we retreated to our corners, I asked myself again if I actually wanted to be married—to anyone. Sometimes it felt like walking barefoot across the desert without a hat. In my first marriage, I'd collected secret hurts like a chipmunk stores a cheek full of nuts while I walked ten steps behind and murmured, "Yes, dear, whatever you'd like," at the appropriate time.

During the long years between the two marriages, I'd worn my hair any damn way I pleased. I'd done anything else I wanted without permission, too. Anything!

I loved to travel, so Jim knew a trip would mend things between us. Since I'd never seen the limestone buildings and fields of dandelions I'd heard so much about in Indiana, I suggested we drive the first leg of the trip from our home in the Florida Panhandle to the small town south of Indianapolis where his best friend lived. I could have suggested we hitchhike and Jim would have agreed. After a visit with his friend, we'd tour the center of the country. The trip was huge; we'd be gone for six weeks. But as I'd reminded Jim, he had a lot to make up for.

* * *

I'd never uttered a word to Jim about Sadie, so it seemed odd, as Lucy and I stood together at the window, that I entertained the idea of telling her about my sister. Something about Lucy made me think that I could. In the past, I saw women as threats. They were either too rich or too thin or too beautiful, all of the things that I was not, so I'd steered clear of them as much as possible. Our mother had died when Sadie was ten and I was eleven. Since we had no one to teach us the woman thing, I learned on my own. If manipulating and backstabbing became part of it, so be it. I was doing the best I could. When I tried looking into their heads, what I saw there told me they didn't trust me anymore than I trusted them. Plus, they were famous for saying inane things like, "Oh, you look so cute in that outfit," which made me want to reply, "Sugar, at fifty, cute isn't what we're aiming for."

Lucy seemed to be someone I could trust, someone who didn't have an agenda. But even so, I decided I wouldn't tell her about Sadie. I'd just met Lucy, which meant I needed to look good in her eyes. I knew that when I talked about Sadie and what had happened, I always came off looking like the despicable person I was.

Still, I had to wonder if Lucy ever questioned her marriage or even the idea of abortion, as I did. Or was she always as assured as she appeared now? At this early hour, she was exquisite in the harsh, unkind light of the kitchen, even without makeup. On the outside she was perfect, except for a tiny raspberry birthmark in the curve of her neck that she worried now with a thumbnail, her only sign that anything was amiss.

When I thought about it, from the outside looking in, I probably seemed self-assured, too. It was all in the presentation. A smile that hoped to please, a decent hair-do, the right causes. As a woman's libber, I'd burned my bra with the best of them. On the question of abortion, I was on the right side. I knew the words. "It's not about right or wrong, it's about choice." But only ninety-nine percent of me believed that for sure. So I was left with one percent that wasn't so sure, and the ruckus of that one percent sometimes played havoc with me.

I'd always wanted children, but Sadie was the fertile one in our family. Plus, she was my father's favorite, even before the awful accident that left her with a limp and never let him forget he'd been driving when he shouldn't have been. Things like that could eat at you, especially if you were a willful child as I was, who wanted things her way and who, even now, had trouble seeing past the end of her own nose. Some people were born good. I was not one of those people. I was not a good person. The older I got, the more this bothered me, but not enough to stop me from doing the things I shouldn't. The important thing was keeping them under the radar, at which I was an expert. Then they didn't count.

"Why do you keep getting pregnant?" I'd yelled at Sadie. "You know better."

" . . . in the heat of passion," Sadie had answered dreamily as if she were reading lines from a Harlequin novel.

With each of her abortions, the one percent had kicked in and made me wonder if I had the percentages wrong. Somehow the subject had become twisted in my mind. It stopped being about Sadie and abortion and became about Sadie and me. Every baby she decided not to have, had become the baby I couldn't have.

My own abortion had been about the wrong time, wrong man, wrong place. It had fallen into a category all its own.

"They're here whether Logan is at home or not," Lucy said.

"So they're here every day?"

"Every day."

"I'm sure knowing the legal ins and outs, what's off limits and what's not, is important," I said.

"Very."

With a stunning nonchalance, she slid a tray from a cabinet and set up two cups, sugar, cream. "I'll take them coffee. The women usually have a cup. In their eyes, I'm not a baby killer," she went on. "I'm only married to one, so it's nothing personal with them."

I stared at her as if she'd suddenly sprouted two heads. How could she do that? I listened to the clink of the cups on the tray, watched her pour. Then I asked myself the question that really baffled me: *Why would she want to?*

"Colin is a different story."

"Colin?"

"The man with the saxophone. He was our neighbor once, a college professor, who lived right there." She leaned toward the window and pointed next door at the house with the gray mansard roof. "He plays in a band now."

"Oh?" I said with a raised eyebrow.

"He wouldn't drink my coffee if his life depended on it. To him, that would betray the cause. In his eyes, I'm guilty by association."

"Really?"

"Really. We're sinners, Logan and I. Colin is here to save our souls." She stopped with the coffee pot poised over a cup. "Haughty ambition for someone whose own soul is in jeopardy, wouldn't you say?" She set the coffee pot down on the counter and without waiting for me to answer, went on. "Before he *got saved.*" She bracketed the two words in air quotes. "When he and Mary lived next door, one of his students had an abortion. After the scandal destroyed his marriage and teaching career at the college, it seemed a good time to repent and be born again."

"Do you believe in that?

"No, but he does. Hell can be a frightening place, I suppose, when you suddenly think you might wind up there."

I glanced outside at the man who had caused such chaos in the lives of others, noting how mild and nonthreatening he appeared. Then I remembered how the women stepped back when he arrived and gave way to him and his music. I had to wonder about that. What gave him such power? Had the women handed it over to him as his sacred right, or had he brought it with him in his convertible along with the sax, tossing it in casually into the backseat at the last minute like an afterthought?

While Lucy delivered the coffee outside, I stepped down into the sitting area off the kitchen. Huge patio windows flanked the back of the house and sunlight flooded the sprawling area. At home, Jim left the blinds pulled in our dayroom until I wanted to scream and finally did. "You move to Florida to live in the sunshine, then sit all day with the blinds closed!"

"It's safe to say we're still adjusting to each other, would you agree?" he'd answered kindly.

And as much as I understood what a nice guy Jim was and how I'd hate to lose him, there I went again, trudging across the desert. Don't look back, just keep walking.

The sun, brilliantly gold and dazzling, set afire the wind chimes that lined the eaves of the house. Red birds in etched glass, capiz shells, copper moons and stars, whimsical teddy bears and pink balloons in painted metals. I'd never seen so many of them in one place. At the back of the house and away from the racket out front, the air was stirred by their tinkle and spin. They flashed in the sunlight, doing their best to drown out the noisy saxophone.

Lucy and I took our coffee to the sitting area that faced the patio and pool. Warblers crowded the bird feeder, pecked industriously for a few seconds, then scurried away. At the far edge of the yard, the swimming pool, drained for resurfacing, sat scooped out and eerily empty. I stared at the huge, yawning gray hole and was reminded of the belly of a whale.

"Does it bother you that Colin thinks you're a sinner?" I asked when we were settled.

Romeo had come to nuzzle her knees and she looked up from where she'd leaned to scratch behind his ears. "Colin isn't the only one in town who feels that way," she said. "He's just the only one who's brave enough to stand outside and taunt us."

"So everyone knows that Logan does abortions?"

"In a town like this one? Of course."

"That must be hard."

"Well, sure, no one likes being shunned."

"Would it be easier if nobody knew?

"What do you mean?"

"I just—"

Before I could finish, she interrupted. "Oh, Cele, do you think I'm ashamed of Logan? I'm not. I'm proud of what he does."

"I didn't mean . . . just that sometimes. . ." I stammered, then stopped. That's exactly what I meant. For me, 'it' only counted if you got caught—'it' being any number of things like the scene out front that in my book had 'caught' written all over it.

Generously, she let the moment pass. "He's traveled for about fifteen years. It was hardest at first, when our old friends gave us the cold shoulder. Oh, I was still on the library board, and the dress shop downtown was happy for my business, but invitations to social events dried up. We were no longer invited to Christmas parties or backyard barbecues. Suddenly, we were lepers. Logan needed their approval more than I did, so it helped that he traveled so much. After about five years, it got easier. We met new friends who'd moved into town." She smiled. "And we have each other. There's always that."

I remembered Jim telling me they were both married to someone else when they met. I thought of how Logan had looked at her last evening and how envious I was of the look. It had devoured her as if she were a spoonful of something delicious. I could understand why she'd fallen in love with him.

We stayed in close touch with Lucy and Logan—emails, trips back and forth, several vacations together. Later, I thought back to that morning when she and I had sipped coffee and listened to the music of the wind chimes together. How could we have known that in just a few years, both Jim and Logan would be gone and what was to come?

Two years after that first visit, Jim died of lung cancer, a fast-growing kind that seemed to sweep him away. Last week, Logan died of a heart attack when so many do not in this age of stents and clot busters. The previous October, he had attended the small private service for Jim. Lucy hadn't come. Her mother had been critically ill at the time.

Now, with pink peonies hanging from their stems like bashful heads of lettuce, I'm back in Indiana for Logan's funeral. I hadn't intended to come, but Lucy insisted. I'm still scratching my head trying to figure out why I said yes. My usual mode of operation is to run the other way.

At the church, she and I sit in the front pew together. She and Logan had no children or relatives other than a niece and several cousins scattered across the country. As the widow of Logan's best friend, I suppose I'm the next best thing to kin.

The minister, a solemn man who says as ministers do when they've never set eyes on the deceased they are eulogizing, ". . .although I wasn't fortunate enough to have the privilege to know Logan in this life. . ."lest we, the family and friends of the deceased, make the erroneous presumption that Logan was a churchgoer.

"I'm never quite sure why they always feel it necessary to include that." I lean close to Lucy and whisper louder than I intended.

With her back as straight as a plumb line, she says quietly, "At least he left out the part about the mistress."

"Mistress?" I ask, shocked that she knows.

"Yes. It's surprising what you find out about them once they're gone."

I take a deep breath, let it out slowly and turn to listen to the minister.

After the funeral, Lucy and I drive together from the church to the family's ancient log cabin in Brown County for the burial. I listen cautiously while she tells me about Logan's affair.

"I discovered it while going through his belongings. He wasn't as careful as he should have been. Credit card receipts can be damning. They're all from the Jacksonville area, so that's where she must live," Lucy explains. She pauses, then says, "I can't imagine why I'm so shocked. After all, I stole him from someone else. What did I expect?" She fingers the raspberry birthmark nestled like a tiny bruise in the fine lines of her neck. "I hated that. It always stayed with me, what I'd done." Her beautiful skin is sallow now and she presses her fingers against her lips, holding back tears. I feel sorry for her, for her loss.

In a moment, with her composure restored, she goes on, "I'm glad we resurfaced the pool. It makes the house easier to sell."

I think of how lovely the pool was this morning surrounded by banks of terra cotta pots that drip with blossoms, sunlight dancing across the face of the water. What had surprised me about the gutted pool two years ago was how the sides had been dull, mud-colored cement that was rough and uneven. Back then, only the bright rim of decorative tiles around the top was slick and smooth. Even though Logan had explained how draining it took several days, I envisioned an enormous bucket, moving slowly up and down, emptying bucket after bucket of sun-filled water.

"The money is gone. Between Logan's bad investments and his frivolous spending on the woman, nothing is left," Lucy says quickly. "I was lucky to get a job at the university. Fancy me going from patron of the children's museum to a housemother at a university dorm. If you're wondering, that's called letting the air out of one's ego."

I try to still my mind and keep it focused on what's in front of us—the narrow winding road, the white oak and ash trees that close around us. I think of how I didn't really walk ten steps behind in my first marriage. It only felt like I did. "I see you're still distributing yourself equally to everyone," my husband had yelled. "If you didn't want to get caught having the abortion, why did you use this?" he'd yelled, waving the credit card bill in my face.

When I'd said, "It could have been yours," he'd simply given me a withering look and turned away.

* * *

Outside of the car now, thick stands of oaks on each side of the highway drape us in a canopy of green. In the dim interior, the only sound in the silence is the faint thump of the concrete breaks in the pavement. Lucy is quiet. She doesn't tell me how she'll go on, if she'll live in anger or regret. At this point, does she even know? I try not to wonder why she's waited until today to tell me about the mistress.

When my sister and I used to snitch coins from our mother's purse, Sadie, her tongue purple from grape popsicle, was the one who got caught. "You didn't tell on me?" she'd asked. "Nope!" I'd assured her. And I hadn't. But if I'd been found out, I would have told on her. I knew that. Even then, I knew that. But I never had to worry since Sadie was always the one who was caught. As for me, the one who took the easy way out, I always got off scot free.

I push the shameful and humiliating things I've done to the back of my mind, something, with practice, I've become skilled at. They disappear, like sliding a letter into an envelope and sealing the flap.

As we round the last curve leading to the cabin, the music of the wind chimes rushes over us. They dangle like necklaces from the tulip tree, the red oak, the front porch eves. The sound is a melancholy ache that settles over the gathering of family and friends that greets us in the clearing.

A banker type man in a fine blue business suit with an appropriately somber countenance steps toward Lucy. After being ostracized by the community for standing up heroically for what she believes, she submits to his embrace with a dignity and grace that I've come to expect of her. I am clueless about how she manages to pull this off.

I don't belong in the circle that surrounds her now. Instead, I linger beside the front porch where Prince and Romeo lie stretched out, surveying the crowd with lazy eyes. Suddenly, a brown wren flits through the thick underbrush nearby. It seems to remind Romeo of his purpose and he struggles to stand. Once on his feet, he raises his front paw and plunges his snout forward in an elegant pose.

I've been successful at sealing away the mean and hateful things I've done—except for two. One is the hateful word I said to Sadie, a word I can't take back now that she's gone. "A barren Sadie isn't a bad thing," I'd said, seething in my anger and frustration at yet another pregnancy and abortion, her third, a botched one this time. The part that was left inside of her was spit out finally like a mouthful of tainted meat. I'd said this before we knew it would be her last, before we knew it would be the one that killed her.

Romeo holds his proud stance while I am left forever with that hateful and archaic word, a word I knew I'd used for dead, clinging like sawdust to my tongue.

Now another deed I can't take back sits like a painful stab wound in my chest. Reaching for the porch post, I steady myself. I take deep breaths, in and out, in and out. With each breath, the pain is sharp and urgent. A scream wells up and I clamp my lips together to hold it inside. I lean my forehead against the tree trunk and welcome the brittle bite of the bark.

When I hear the pine-needle crunch of footsteps around the corner of the cabin, I turn to see a man approach tentatively. He keeps to himself, stopping several yards away. I lean closer for a better look. Can it be? Yes, the man is Colin, but a different Colin from before, so changed I hardly recognize him. His hair is brushed into a slick neat helmet. He seems subdued, but restless and uncomfortable, his eyes roaming the gathering of people. When he sees Lucy, he takes a step forward, then stops.

Glancing over, Lucy sees him and separates herself from the crowd. Once beside him, she reaches out and touches his arm. I am stilled by this simple touch, so stilled the rush of my blood seems to stop, too. Inside of her is a goodness I do not know. When she smiles up at Colin, I stand in the stillness of the moment and hold close the goodness and the hope I see there.

Her simple gesture is like hearing the words "I love you" when you've done something unforgivable. It makes me want to cry, *I am sorry, I am so very sorry.*

I don't cry out now and won't. What's the point in that? But suddenly I understand why I've come back. I'm here because I'm banking on the decency in Lucy to be contagious. The truth that's always been there, but that I've never admitted to myself before, is that the awful things we do in life do count. They always count, whether we're caught or not.

For now, I ask only of myself that I stand in the promise of that moment to come.

A CRAZY PATCHWORK QUILT

MELISSA THREATENS TO quit work here at the nursing home and go back to decorating cakes at Merita. When I laugh, she stretches a pillowcase taut, flicks my arm and leaves it stinging. "Just wait," she tells me. "One day I'll send you a sheet cake by Overnight Express with cabbage roses as big as grapefruits on top that says, 'See, I told you so.'"

It's hot in the laundry room. I fold a towel still warm from the dryer in half, then again in quarters. "I can make twelve-fifty an hour there and breathe better, too," she tells me. Her boyfriend, Leonard Beaker, shot her in the chest when she was eighteen. She's thirty-six now and Leonard is sixty-five. Ever since the gunshot, she's had an awful time catching her breath. The air here at the We-Kare, heavy with disinfectant and cleaning solutions, gets to her, although the sluggish humidity outside is sometimes as bad. When she wheeled Mr. Larson out on the sun porch yesterday, the heat left her gasping. Once, while we were changing Mrs. Garvey, Melissa bent over the bed too far and cut her wind off completely. Pursing her lips, she made a hissing noise that sounded like a slow leak in a tire. When she recovered, she jerked up her blouse and pointed to the long scar wrapped around her rib cage. "The shot went in here," she said, as though she had to convince me it had really happened. "See that little pucker of skin?

That's where they put the tube when the lung filled up with blood." She finished with a wheeze.

"I believed you all the time," I told her soothingly.

Melissa's world is a rich collage of sounds, colors and motion, while mine seems somehow fixed in time. I picture my mother, dusting her rose bushes in the side yard, and try to imagine how she'd react to learn that I know someone in real life with a gunshot wound in her chest—plus someone who wore orange and red and stripes and paisley mixed.

Appearances have always been so important to Mama. Although Mama has grown accustomed to them now, she was once appalled by the cumbersome crepe sole lace-ups I wear "to work outside the home."

When she tells Mrs. Taylor at the A & P how I work at the We-Kare merely to give myself something to do, I cover my mouth with my hand to smother a cough. I don't have the heart to remind her that what I make here, together with the meager income from the tiny Atwood trust fund, barely keep us afloat. Her checks from Social Security help, too, but altogether, it's barely enough to keep up our big house and all that goes with it. I've let the help go except for Hannah, who still comes in on Tuesday afternoons to take Mama to the beauty parlor. For the trip downtown, Mama wears mismatched athletic socks and canvas tennis shoes I buy off the rack at Kmart. I hear her explain to Hannah how the shoes caress her arches like the high fashion pumps she once wore from I. Miller's. I'm surprised she remembers. Mama hasn't ordered her shoes from Atlanta for a long time now.

For Melissa, however, where her shoes come from is of little importance. "Long as they don't mash my bunions or rub blisters on my heels when I do a jive step, I couldn't care less whose name's branded on the instep," she says, doing a quick boogie across the polished tile in the diet kitchen.

Melissa says she and Leonard have been together for as long as she can remember. She tells her son, Harry Lee—whose father she's careful to point out is not Leonard—he shouldn't hit people. "Look what happened to me," she tells him. "You can't trust what they'll do once you hit them."

As she relates their conversation to me, I lift an eyebrow, puzzled about what she's saying. Did she hit Leonard first? Harry Lee appears to understand. A freshman discus thrower at Savannah State, he hasn't been shot once.

Before I met Melissa, I thought someone with that name would be tiny with delicate hands, a pure white half-moon at the base of each slender tapering nail, and the fragrance of gardenias wafting about her in the air. This Melissa is big-boned and massive, with skin so smooth I think of sleek taffy left a fraction too long in the pan, then pulled a rich honey gold. Her nails are wide, blunt as fence posts, and she smells tartly of freshly-picked limes. Often she moves through the corridors at the We-Kare like a gigantic wind-up toy, or some lumbering NBA player sailing a balled-up piece of paper into a trash can at the far corner of the room. She leaves a stirring in her wake that settles only after she's left the dayroom. I imagine Mama watching her bounce about and then saying, "For a heavy person, she's certainly light on her feet."

Herman, the laundry man, bumps into Melissa from behind with a linen hamper full of dirty towels. She turns smartly, explains to him where he can go, beginning immediately, and tells him specifically what he can do with his laundry cart on the way. Once, answering the front door of the We-Kare, she found a bedraggled man begging for quarters. "Get a job, brother," she'd said brusquely. "There's no reason why you can't. You notice I work, and although I know this'll be a shock to your system, so does most everybody else."

Yet when I look into Melissa's eyes, brown and shiny as dark chocolate cordials, a hint of lavender shading each lid, and watch her strip a bed in one graceful swoop, I am reminded of nimble hoofs prancing about, lithe as a tap dancer. Somehow, then, the name Melissa fits.

* * *

"I've got somebody," she sings. She points my way. "You need
somebody, too." I don't tell her that once, I almost did. I think
back to Mama, her spine straight as a plumb line, pouring tea at
the wrought iron table on the screened-in back porch. Across
from her sat Peter Brown, a linen napkin draped across his knee,
fidgeting nervously. She liked my young man, she told me later.
Yet when he left that day, she began making plans to have his
teeth fixed. And as I cleared the table, I heard her at the silver
chest in the dining room, counting the flatware.

The next day I sat across from Peter in McDonald's, my arms
sweaty, sticky against the tabletop. He touched the braid that
rested against my shoulder like a thick ginger-colored rope. When
he trailed his fingertip gently down the plane of my nose and
across my freckled cheek, I wanted to stop his hand, hold it
against my skin. I knew that if I didn't, I wouldn't see him again.
Then I thought, *What on earth would I do in the mountains of North
Carolina? What on earth would I do with Mama?"* So I left my hands
cupped together on the table in front of me.

I like my work here at the We-Kare. Together Mrs. Lehman and I
watch *As The World Turns* in the dayroom every afternoon, her
smile coy and secretive as if we're doing something risqué when I
spoon a section of grapefruit into her mouth and catch a drop of
juice gliding down her chin. Best of all, I like to hear Melissa talk
about her world. "And then?" I'll ask like an eager child. "What
happened next?"

Before her job at the We-Kare, Melissa sold cypress knee lamps
for a sharp-eyed gypsy at the flea market. She also sorted clothes
in a laundry but quit in the middle of the shift when a butcher
knife with a twelve inch blade fell out of a bloody sheet that had
come from the best funeral home in town. "Can you imagine what
you'd find in sheets from the *second* best? Talk about gruesome!"
she'd said with a shudder.

I laughed when I pictured her springing back as the knife plunged from the spattered sheet to the floor.

Next to decorating cakes at Merita, Melissa says she likes it here at the nursing home best. But for the low pay and not being able to breathe, this job would come in first. "These old people keep you on your toes," she says. "I learn a lot about them from the way they hold the thermometer in their mouth when I take their temperature. The ones who roll it around under their tongues are the easiest to get along with. But Lordy me, you have to watch out for those who clamp down on it and won't open up when the buzzer goes off. They're something else again. You take that peppery Mr. Yarborough, who clinches it between his teeth like it's an old stogie. He's hell on wheels. He makes everybody on Corridor B march in step to occupational therapy like he's a frigging general in the United States Army."

"Not in front of the patients," I caution her in a loud whisper.

"Well, it's the truth. And him nothing but a retired postman."

"Still . . ."

I watch Melissa toss her head, undeterred. I envy her certainty, her abandon, so different from my way—a more hesitant, standing-away-from rather than the jostling-for-position-up-front that I see in her.

When the struts on Harry Lee's truck wear out, Melissa calls Leonard to send money to Savannah for repairs, but he has to think about it first. Melissa waits, patient on the phone while he does. When Leonard is the one to call her and I answer, his speech is flavored with a stilted old world rhythm, but his sound is firm, too. I love to listen to the soft rasp of his speech, which makes me think of mellow bourbon mixed with sparkling branch water. Sometimes we talk while we wait for Melissa to pick up. He tells me how his pension check was lost in the mail, how in the fall he hopes to hunt deer at his old home place off I-10 near Marianna.

A softness creeps into Melissa's voice when she speaks to Leonard, a gentleness that isn't there otherwise. When I hear them talking, I wonder if I shouldn't have elbowed my way into life more eagerly. Something exists between them, a connection, a current surging back and forth that I haven't known, standing at the edge of life as I've done. Together, on her afternoon off, the two of them search for a terrycloth cap trimmed with sprigs of blue heather for Mrs. Nelson. She's bald from the chemo they gave to shrink the lump in her breast, but in her ears she wears tiny earrings shaped like cowboy boots from her sister in El Paso.

Melissa fingers the ridges along Mrs. Nelson's naked scalp, slides the cap into place to cover the bareness. "It was the earrings that did it," she tells me later. "I couldn't stand to think of them dangling next to that head, slick as a gourd." Her eyes shine then, brighter than before. "Good people get cancer," she says with a dry laugh. "You and me, we don't have to worry."

Melissa told me once how she'd spent time in prison for dealing coke. "Can you believe? My boyfriend at the time was a policeman. For all the good that did me," she'd chuckled. "He dealt and snorted right along with me."

When Melissa talks, I think of a crazy patchwork quilt made up of crisp, bright colors but soft ones, too, with vast blank spaces scattered about. Leonard is one color, of course, a mellow blue perhaps, and Harry Lee another. He's doing well at Savannah State. Melissa keeps her fingers crossed that he doesn't fall in love and get some girl pregnant. He and Leonard spread across most of the quilt, but interrupting their bold squares are other splashes of color as well—the policeman, Harry Lee's father.

Lately, Melissa has talked about a wild Cajun named Hap, who lives across the street in a double-wide and rides a black Harley Davidson. He has a heart with an arrow tattooed on his left forearm and a rambling rose design circles the commode seat in his bathroom. Melissa says she loves the way the blossoms climb the back of the lid. "He sleeps on a waterbed in the living room in front of his new twenty-nine inch Zenith," she tells me.

I wonder how she knows.

* * *

I don't think much of it on Monday when Melissa doesn't show up for work—she does that occasionally. Calling them her "mental health days," she'll come back the next morning breathing easy, full of cope. When she misses Tuesday as well, though, I begin to wonder if something is wrong. When I called her house, the phone just rang and rang.

In the cool of late evening, I bike up the hill to Carmen Circle and tap tentatively on the front door of her bungalow. The Bradford pear beside the porch is alive with tiny buds, and pots of scarlet geraniums sit like bookends on either side of the front door. A stillness permeates the place and gives it a feeling of being deserted. Just as I think that perhaps I shouldn't be there at all, a man answers the door, his skin tan and deeply lined like pleats in a length of burlap. He wears a questioning look on his face.

I've developed a picture of Leonard in my mind's eye, first from listening to Melissa, then from talking with him on the phone. I think of him as a man-sized Melissa, muscle bound and fierce, a man with great authority who towers over their lives. The man standing in the doorway, so short I have to look down to meet his eyes, is like nothing I imagined.

"Leonard? It's me, Lizbet, from the We-Kare."

"She's not here," he says, peering up through the screen. "She's gone. Left with Hap on Sunday." He turns, looks past me through the live oaks sprawling across the front yard. His voice now is less firm and mellow than when I've talked with him on the phone. It holds an edge that hasn't been there before. I follow his gaze toward the pink trailer parked across the street, its trim like bright blue piping. As we stand in silence, I think again of the crazy patchwork quilt and all the missing squares.

Over tall glasses of sweet tea at the kitchen table, he says, "As you know, for some while now Hap has lusted in his heart for Melissa." I want to jump in and say, "No, I didn't know." But instead I keep quiet and listen as he goes on. "When she wheeled

81

the lawn mower out of the garage late Saturday afternoon and found a diamond-backed rattler coiled in the blades, Hap, of course, was Johnny-on-the-Spot to help. He fished out the snake with the handle of a hoe. You'd have thought he was a storm trooper with his black sleeveless vest and his flashing tattoo. On top of that," he sips his tea and continues, "for nothing but to show off, he twirled that snake around and around his head like a bull whip while Melissa ducked and screamed, and I watched from behind the screened door. With a snap of his wrist, he flipped the snake's head off on the mailbox beside the curb. That head cracked against the metal so hard, I swear, it sounded like the cap popping off a bottle of 7-Up."

As Leonard speaks, his voice sharpens, quickening with eagerness. I listen, mesmerized. It's as if I stand with him behind the screened door and hear the *twang, twang* as the snake streaks through the heavy air. I am so caught up in the story that when the snake whistles past Melissa's face, I jump with her as the head hits the side of the mailbox.

"Hap draped the dead snake, still quivering, across the chain link fence as if he was hanging out clothes to dry," Leonard goes on more slowly, solemnly now in that stilted formal tone. "Then he threw his arm across Melissa's shoulder and suggested—loud enough for me to hear, I might add—that the two of them go inside his trailer and do it in the living room on his waterbed in front of his new twenty-nine inch Zenith."

I glance down quickly away from Leonard's eyes and think of the rose buds circling Hap's commode.

"At that point, I yelled, 'Come in here, Melissa!'," Leonard adds grimly, his face engraved in deep creases. "When I said that, she looked over at me funny like she was a little girl and I'd called her inside to punish her for something naughty." But he is not finished. "Then she laughed and pushed Hap's arm away. When she got even with me in the doorway, she gave me a little shove. 'You can't raise me and fuck me, too, Leonard,' she said. The next morning, the two of them were gone."

The late afternoon sun lies in slanted rays across the table in front of us, like spokes in a tilted wheel. I think of Melissa after she's talked with Leonard on the phone, how she strolls Mrs. Berman out to the sun porch in the heat without complaining, sits with her while she watches the sunset.

After finishing his story, Leonard is like someone at a crossroad who's mislaid his road map and can't remember which way to turn. As I watch him, now spent, I wonder what made him feel he must take me back so vividly to her leaving. Still, I have to ask. "And you let her go?"

He brightens. "Oh, she'll be back," he says, cocking an eyebrow.

I study the raised brow, the sudden lift of his shoulders. Is there something about the story that I've missed? How can he be so sure that she'll come back? I think of the thing that keeps them together, that connection I've felt before and never understood. Can it be explained by Hap and their leaving together or is it something more than that? Is it all the things that have gone before—the pucker of skin sitting like a pair of pursed lips on the side of Melissa's chest, Harry Lee and her need for him to succeed, the gentleness that is there when she talks with Leonard on the phone? Would I know the answer if I had chosen a mountaineer from Pigeon Forge rather than faded tea cozies and night blooming jasmine?

Suddenly I understand: I'm not one of those people who could have chosen otherwise. I'll never be someone who surrenders herself with such abandon. I'm stingy, hoarding my spirit like we hoard family recipes. For me, reaching out for something more means the possibility of losing what I have. And God forbid, what happens if there's not enough to go around. I've thought pride kept me from being a chance-taker. What on earth would people think? But that's a Mama thing. For me, it's more than that. For several years now, I've seen only the thrill and excitement of Melissa's world, a world that's richly lived. Now, I see the messiness that's there, too, and feel myself withdrawing into the safety of my own tidy life. It's courage I lack, courage to deal with the dirty parts, like mud tracks on the parlor rug. Mama's not to blame. She's been my excuse for choosing to peer over the edge rather than take the chance I'd dirty my hands trying to climb inside, but if I'm honest, I have to admit I'm the one who chose to settle for less.

"You'll tell her to call me," I say when I am outside, straddling my bike.

"I'll tell her."

As I ride away, crickets begin their busy *chirp, chirp* down by the creek at the foot of the hill. The wheels of my bike scatter a whirlwind of oak leaves circling near the ground. I glance over my shoulder. The snake's head has left a smudge on the mailbox between the "a" and "e" in Beaker. From a distance, it looks like rust, but closer up, it had fit in like an extra letter.

The afternoon sunlight plays across Leonard's bent shoulders as he leans forward and scrapes at the spot on the side of the mailbox with a callused thumb.

IN THE PALM
OF MAMA'S HAND

MAMA SAYS SHE hopes whoever gets the baby won't name her Shawn or Dawn or Tara, one of those "era names," as she calls them, the kind that marks a generation, or worse yet, something like Dakota or Satchel or Moonbeam.

I sit beside her in the front seat of the car and listen to her over the rhythm of the wipers and "Muskrat Love" on the radio. The wipers swish back and forth with a sloppy *slap, slap*. It's Wednesday afternoon. We're on our way to see Miss Lawson, the family guidance counselor in Macon.

"That is, if Mary Jo decides to give up the baby, of course."

I watch Mama out of the corner of my eye but don't answer. She doesn't expect me to, since she's talking to herself and not to me anyway. When she's on a diet, she has a habit of patting her stomach as if to say, "What, you're not gone yet? And me living on nothing but celery and lettuce for two straight days."

She jerks the steering wheel and the car veers, splashing through water pooled on the highway. She's nervous today. I can tell by the tone of her voice. It's reached what Daddy calls her "female static pitch"—each word sharp and crowded close to the next one, like static crackling on a radio.

I'll say this for her. She's run up against some situations she can't handle, and for once, she's swallowed her pride and asked for help. As she likes to point out, these are situations not even mentioned in *A Southern Belle Primer*.

I listen hard when Mama talks about the *Primer*. I'm almost twelve and smart for my age, but I never know if she's kidding or not. The *Primer* goes into explicit detail, she says, about how every belle should own at least one deviled egg dish, plus a cut-crystal punch bowl with twelve cups and a ladle to match. But not one word about a daughter due to deliver in four months without benefit of wedlock and another daughter set to wed a scant two months later.

On top of this, the *Primer* fails to shed light on how to handle the groom, a senior at a respected school like Emory, who's suddenly lost his mind. With engraved invitations ordered and the Magnolia Room at the Wellington Heights Country Club reserved for the reception, he has the nerve to say, "No sirree, I'm not setting foot inside the door of a place that's racist and doesn't serve blacks."

According to Mama, Kevin chose to make this announcement at the worst possible place—in front of God and everybody at the big cookout two weeks ago thrown by none other than the president of the bank. Mama said she took a deep breath and scanned the guest list quickly in her mind. Of course, she knew even before she began the color line hadn't been crossed. At this ungodly hour, with everything settled, did Kevin think she should sprinkle in a few of another color? The very idea! "As if that has anything to do with getting married and having a grand party to celebrate the occasion," she said to him. "I think we're talking apples and oranges here, Kevin. Please!"

Mama speeds up. Outside the downpour has almost stopped.

"Where Kevin gets these ideas is beyond me. I told your daddy, we're being exposed to a side of the father of our future flesh-and-blood that's frightening. You might not admire every gene in your own family, but at least you're familiar with what they are."

The rain turns to a mist, a hazy fog that shrouds the windshield. When I ride in a car with the windows closed tight and the damp and chill safely outside, a cozy feeling closes around me like there's nothing in the world but me and the car and the rain.

Mama says the same thing happens to her. She says she feels as if she's wrapped safe and snug in a soft cocoon. The other members of the family aren't with us. Daddy is at the *Herald* office putting the paper to bed. He told us later someone tried to assassinate President Ford that day in Sacramento. Beth's at Valdosta State, and Mary Jo has dropped out of Emory and is at home with her feet propped on a hassock to keep down the swelling. But Mama says she feels like she can reach out and touch them and know that they're safe, too.

We turn onto the old Trestle Road. Outside live oaks arch overhead like the ceiling of some grand cathedral. They make me think of a game Mama used to play with us when we were little. She'd lock her hands together with her fingers tucked inside her palms, except for her index fingers. They were left sticking straight up in the air.

"Here's the church, here's the steeple, open the door and here's the people," she'd sing and flip open her hands. Inside her fingers would be wrapped around each other, all mixed up in a jumble.

Beside the highway, the trees begin to thin. Towering loblollies replace the sprawling oak and beneath the pines, the ground is covered in a slick carpet of needles. I curl my legs beneath me and settle in to listen. I'm what Mama calls her "sounding board." She talks to me when she needs to lay out something and look at it in words. In my mind's eye, I see her line each word up for inspection and give it a little shake as if to say, "Let's see. Are your ears clean? Did you brush your teeth? Is your homework done?" She says I'm impartial, which is more than she can say for her other two daughters. They're closer together in age and always on the same side, which means, nine times out of ten, against Mama.

Except for this time. This time, it's Mama and Beth against Mary Jo. They both think she should give up the baby for adoption. So far, Mary Jo has agreed to nothing— which is why we're on our way to the Family Counseling Center.

Mary Jo is nineteen and her baby is due the second week of April. Elizabeth Ann—Beth for short and the bride-to-be—is twenty-one. Since I was born so much later, I'm referred to as the change-of-life baby. Every time Mama sees Ruth Ann Marshall, who is in my class at school and slow, she gives me a big hug. "Oh, Ashley, I'm so grateful you can count to ten and tie your shoes right."

So I don't get a big head, she goes on to explain that just because I'm not retarded does not, by any means, imply that I'm perfect. "You have a full dose of stubbornness, from your father's side of the family, of course."

Genes are important to Mama. That's why she's so concerned about Kevin.

"Oh, Carolyn," Daddy says to Mama. "I wouldn't worry if I were you. Remember? You worried that our girls might have Aunt Ruby's disposition and look how things turned out. I'm surrounded by three beautiful young women who walk like me and talk like me and look like you."

Actually, even though Daddy likes to think that true, it's not. Mary Jo looks like him. She's the swan in the family—tall and thin with a slim neck, a knockout in turtlenecks. Even with her face puffy and her skin splotchy from being pregnant, she's still beautiful. If the sun hits the auburn streaks in her blonde hair just right, it fairly sparkles. When I was little and what she called a nuisance, I lost a shell earring she'd bought in Hilton Head. She was so mad, she wouldn't tow me on her bike to the Tenneco for a solid week. Even with a scowl on her face, I never stopped thinking she was pretty enough for the cover of *Teen*.

On top of that, she's smart, too. While Beth and I struggle along making Bs and Cs, Mary Jo brings home straight As every time. Still, Mama says she thinks Beth and I get more bounce out of life than Mary Jo does. She's not as quick to laugh as we are. Mama says when she was little, people were forever telling her they'd never seen such solemn eyes on a little girl before.

Beth takes after Mama's side of the family. They're both on diets because of the wedding. Mama's short and dumpy with a high waistline that makes her belts ride up in front.

"I've been fighting the same ten pounds for fifteen years," she says. Weight-wise, if you're interested, she can take you back decades.

I pull the sun visor down and fumble in my pocketbook for my lipstick. If I use a pale pink and put it on light, I'm allowed to wear it. I feel Mama eyeing me to make sure I don't coat it too thick. Daddy doesn't like me wearing it at all. Usually he's on my side but not when it comes to makeup.

Lately he's been acting funny about a lot of things. I can tell he has Mary Jo on his mind. He stands around picking his teeth and peering at her over the rim of his reading glasses with sad, worried eyes.

"I don't ask much of my girls," he'll say. "Only that you keep hair out of the sink and that your mama be here in the evening when I get home from work."

Mama says she's spoiled him by trying to be nice and be there sometimes. Now he expects it all the time.

She turns off the windshield wipers as the sun slides from behind a cloud. "And your daddy says to me, 'I don't see why we don't move the reception to the Holiday Inn if Kevin feels that way about the country club. They do a tasty creamed chicken dish for Rotary every Monday.' So I say in return, 'Will, dear, a reception for three hundred people is hardly the same thing as two dozen men who can't tell the difference between real butter and margarine.'"

I imagine Mama explaining to Daddy in her even-though-I-know-you-won't-understand-I'll-explain-anyway voice. Sometimes she uses it on me.

My foot goes to sleep where I've sat on it, so I swing it out from under me and prop my heel on the dash. There's a tingling in my toes. Traffic picks up on the outskirts of Macon. Narrow two-lane dirt roads wind back toward neat mobile homes in the distance. Tidy lawns with paving stones lead up to the front doors and shrubs nudge the bottoms of the windows, giving the trailers a permanent I'm-here-to-stay look.

"Roxanne just saw Jaws and says it's not scary at all," I tell Mama. "It's at the drive-in. Can we go?" She had already said no once, but you can bet I wasn't giving up that easily.

Ignoring my question, Mama went on. "'Why don't we ask Beth what we should do? After all, it is *her* wedding,' your daddy says back. Sometimes I feel like turning this whole wedding thing over to him. Let him get a taste of what it's like trying to find out-of-season strawberries for the fondue, a salad mold shaped like a wedding bell for the bridesmaid's luncheon, or a pair of blue satin shoes with high insteps that don't crowd my bunion. To say nothing of our obstinate son-in-law-to-be, even if he does come of good stock, with parents who happen to be members of the very country club whose threshold he now refuses to cross."

Mama thinks Beth is in no condition to make a sensible decision about anything at the moment. Her primary concern is what Kevin's mother will think about the maid of honor having a baby with no father in sight. I can see how that would have her rattled. After Beth has a good cry about that, she has to sit down and have another one because she feels guilty about not "being there" for Mary Jo.

Mama says she's thinking of adding another chapter to the *Primer* entitled, "How To Work In A Nervous Breakdown When There's So Much Else To Do." Since she thinks there's something wrong with people who require more than the *Primer* and Reverend Rollins at the First Baptist to solve their problems, asking for help has not been easy for her.

To make matters worse, her first impression of Miss Lawson at the counseling center was shocking.

"Not that I had the least idea of what to expect," Mama told Daddy later. "But an individual with hair like a tangerine halo around her head is the last thing I'd have pictured. Her saving grace was her sensible shoes and her blue suit because the entire time I'm looking at her head, I'm saying to myself, *nobody* is born with hair *that* color."

On page fifty-three of the *Primer*, it states explicitly how there's a fine line between flashy and cheap—and gives examples. Mama said Miss Lawson definitely skirts the divide.

But Mama's fair if she's anything, I'll say that for her. She was the first to admit later that she did a quick turnaround the minute Miss Lawson opened her mouth. In a nutshell, she said to Mama, "If you and Beth continue at the rate you're going, you'll warp Mary Jo's psyche forever."

Mama sat with her skirt tucked tightly around her knees paying close attention. She knew what she was hearing was what she needed to hear. After a while, Miss Lawson's orange hair didn't distract her in the least.

Up to then, even though Mary Jo kept getting bigger and bigger, nobody at our house talked about the baby. Mama made sure Mary Jo stayed off her feet, bought loose-fitting maternity jumpers to wear with her turtlenecks, and fed her multivitamins along with gallons of whole milk. But the only time the baby was mentioned was when Mama and Beth asked Mary Jo if she'd decided whether she was giving it up for adoption.

That first day at the counselor's office, when Mama gave the history, she explained how she and Beth had decided if they didn't talk about the baby, Mary Jo could give it up without hurting so much—if that's what she decided to do.

Miss Lawson said, "Mary Jo is having a baby regardless of what she does with it after it's born. A name should be chosen and the baby treated as a member of the family because that's exactly what it is. This will prepare Mary Jo for what's called a natural grieving process if she does give it up—just as if the baby died."

When Miss Lawson said those words, they seemed to loop in a wide curve over her desk and land with a plop in Mama's lap. She leaned back and took a sharp breath that caught like a sob in the back of her throat. Her hands, laying folded like a deck of cards in her lap, tightened as if hanging on to each other for dear life.

"We weren't trying intentionally to hurt Mary Jo. We didn't know any better," Mama said in the small voice she uses when Grandma Dotson has scolded her. "It's just that . . . there are some things . . . Mary Jo is not as strong as other people." She stopped.

I glanced over at her, wondering what in the world she was talking about.

On the way home, we dropped by the library and checked out *All There Is To Know About Choosing A Name For Your Baby*. I pulled the sun visor down and in the car mirror watched my lips purse in a pink bow when I sounded out the names, just like Miss Roach had taught in elocution class. Cass-an-dra, Mel-ann-ee, Dee-eed-re.

Meanwhile, Mama was busy rehashing what Miss Lawson had said. "She makes the most sense. I just hope if Mary Jo chooses adoption, she doesn't waste one of our good family names on the baby. The people who get it will change it to something they like better anyway." As if she suddenly heard what she was saying, she stopped and side-glanced at me. She was quiet for a minute. She smiled, reached over, and patted my hand. "Well, no matter, lots of good ones to go around. Don't you think? I'm sure they won't all get used up anyway."

Right away, Mama and Beth began putting into practice Miss Lawson's advice. In fact, Beth began sessions with her when she was home from Valdosta State, which was more often as the wedding date drew closer. Finally Mama convinced Mary Jo to come along, too. When she suggested that Daddy join them, he said, "Do I have to? All I want is for Mary Jo to be happy. Tell me what the counselor says I'm supposed to do and I'll do it. No sense in all of us crowding in there."

Me? I kept everybody company on the rides in to Macon to see Miss Lawson. When I was with Mama, I went inside with her for the sessions. With Beth and Mary Jo, I stayed outside in the reception room and thumbed through magazines. Don't ask me why. It was a mystery to me, too.

I hold on tight with both hands as Beth swerves off the interstate close behind a semi with Cane's Trucking printed on the back of it. We've had several days of warm weather, enough for a few green shoots to pop out on the dogwoods, but today is chilly, so Beth has the heater on. I'm sweating so much, I roll a can of Pepsi back and forth across my forehead. The sweat beads on the side of the can feel good against my skin.

"I don't know why, for once, Mama can't accept the fact that different isn't good or bad, it's just different, " Beth says. Looking over at me, she makes a face. "Would you stop that? You're making an awful mess."

Because she's the oldest, she forgets sometimes that she's not my second mama. I drop the can to the floor and nudge it with the toe of my shoe. Beth passes the semi, squeezes in between it and a black sports car with tinted windows. The air brakes on the eighteen-wheeler make a wide sweeping sound that closes down around us. I look back and the driver is shaking his head. Still, he smiles, toots his horn two short honks for me.

"She thinks Kevin has funny ways," I say.

"Which means they're different from hers."

"I'll say."

"I'll tell you something if you don't tell anybody."

"What?'

"Donald Roberts is black."

"Who's that?'

"Kevin's friend from Indiana. He's . . ." she hesitates, glances over at me, ". . . in the wedding."

"Holy shit!" I clamp my hand over my mouth and lean back against the seat. I think of how Kevin has told Mama he won't go to the country club because they don't serve blacks but has neglected to mention one word about his black friend. "She's bound to find out sooner or later."

"I know. He would have been at the engagement party, but couldn't make it down."

"When will he tell her?"

"I don't know. He says he'll just let it happen."

"Uh oh."

"You're telling me!" she says, drumming her hands on the steering wheel in time to "Do It To Me One More Time" playing on the car radio. She doesn't know Mama had forbid me from listening to that song and I wasn't about to tell her.

I look across at her and I think how well she's holding up. I picture all of them jumping around in the palm of Mama's hand and have to ask myself if Kevin will stand up to her about this or if there's room for him in there, too.

As we pull into the parking lot of the counseling center, I realize that we haven't mentioned Mary Jo or the baby once since we got in the car even though they're the whole reason we're here.

At home, everybody is following Miss Lawson's suggestions. We try out names on each other to see which ones fit best. Mary Jo likes the single ones while Daddy likes what he calls "the double digits." We can tell when she feels the baby move. She'll rub her stomach and change whatever position she's in to something else.

From where I stand on the sidelines, everything's going well except for one thing. It seems to me high time that some mention is made of the baby's father. Only once did I hear that subject spoken above a whisper. That was the day she told us she was pregnant.

The evening before, Mary Jo had driven home from Atlanta with Kevin. Since they were both at Emory, they usually rode home together. At the beginning of the year, they came home every weekend together but hadn't in several months, which was unusual. Don't ask me why They never said.

94

Mama said later she could have kicked herself at what happened. She said she should have known something was wrong when Mary Jo went into the bathroom to try on a pair of stirrup pants Mama had picked up for her at Belk's.

"Ordinarily, nobody has a shred of modesty at our house," Mama said. "Suddenly, Mary Jo is closing the bathroom door to change her clothes like she thinks she'll send us into shock if we see her in her underwear."

The next morning, Mary Jo slept late. She was dressed for a walk when she came downstairs. I asked if I could go along and she snapped, "No!" She headed out the back door quickly, the collar of the old pea jacket she'd bought at a rummage sale turned up at the neck.

"What's the matter with her?" I asked.

Beth shrugged. I should have known she'd be no help.

The weather was windy and cold that day. We kept looking for some evidence of spring. Except for the scant green nubs on the dogwoods and the sloping fields of rye, we were surrounded by bleak winter browns and grays. Even so, Mary Jo didn't come back for the longest time. When she did, the collar of her jacket was still turned up and she looked like a newborn baby bird, its head stuck up out of the nest, little and skinny and scared. Her cheeks were pale and thinner than usual with deep half-moon shadows under her eyes. The pea jacket was too big every place but one—that was in the front at the waist where it bulged.

When she sat at the kitchen table, she propped her chin in her hand and watched Daddy peel potatoes at the sink. When he turned toward the table, he spotted Mary Jo for the first time.

"Oh, hon, you want to hand that bowl to me?" he asked.

"No, Daddy," she said quietly, in a voice not her own.

I stood at the kitchen door, watching her. Mama, who'd been setting the table in the dining room, walked over and stood behind me in the door. Beth dropped her pencil. Something in Mary Jo's voice stilled us all.

"I'm going to have a baby in April. Don't bother asking who the father is. He's nobody you know."

We all stared at her. The only sound was the *drip, drip, drip* of the leaky faucet at the sink. Daddy had promised Mama yesterday he'd replace the worn out washer.

Finally, a potato in one hand, the paring knife in the other, Daddy pulled a chair from the table and sat carefully, as though if he jarred either of them, they'd explode and blow us to smithereens.

Mama said, "Oh, my God!" without even noticing she'd taken the Lord's name in vain.

Beth looked ready to cry.

For a minute, Mary Jo acted as if she was about to say something else. She never uttered another word.

"I tried to tell Kevin, it's not that they won't serve blacks at the country club, it's that none of that shade has ever *asked* to be served," Mama tells me on our next trip to see Miss Larson. She's still wrestling with what to do about the reception. "Then Mister-Answer-For-Everything says, 'Julian Hill said when Terence Lamb tried to order a Coke from the bar, he was told to go around to the machine outside on the patio.' So I said, 'Kevin, Terence is hired help, something I view as quite different from an established member.' That young man has some funny ways as far as I'm concerned."

Mama ended with that whenever she was talking about Kevin.

I can see him telling Mama his side of the story. He's tall and looks down at you with the softest gray eyes I've ever seen. But when he gets mad, watch out. The softness leaves and his eyes turn into smoky marbles that glint when he talks. He tried growing a beard last summer, but it came in wispy and thin. He finally gave up and shaved it off. When I asked Beth what it felt like to be kissed by a feather duster, she didn't crack a smile. She's sensitive about Kevin. She says he's his own man, something she admires in a person. Even though it's her wedding, she's staying out of the reception fracas.

Mama says since Beth isn't saying anything, it means she's on Kevin's side. Even though the *Primer* states in no uncertain terms that a wife should support a husband in all instances, Mama says, "Contrary to what Beth might think, she and Kevin aren't yet man and wife." And then she adds, "Being unreasonable is a trait that runs in families, something Beth should take note of."

So nothing is settled. Where the reception will be held is still up in the air.

"If I had it to do over again, I'd have an abortion," Mary Jo tells me. She has trouble fitting behind the wheel of the car. Her stomach is hard and round. I reach over, put my palm flat against her bulge and feel a little flutter. She says the baby gets its foot stuck under her rib cage sometimes and gives her a kick like somebody's stabbing her with a knife.

I try to imagine how that must feel and can't. The closest I can come is to think of how much my stomach hurts when I stuff myself with cheese tortellini at Little Napoli on my birthday or when I have a stitch in my side from running too fast. I wonder when I hear Mary Jo fumbling around in the dark, night after night, if it's because of the baby kicking.

She flips the radio to an oldies station and turns up the volume. She listens to this station every time we go into Macon. I've learned the names of most of the songs. They play "Moon River" a lot. It's on now.

"If you'd had an abortion, Mama would've had a fit."

"She never would have found out."

I look over at Mary Jo. "You'd have lied to her?"

"No. I just wouldn't have told her. "

I sit back, think about that one for a while.

"You know why she and Beth think I should give it up?"

"'Cause they think you're too young?"

"No."

"Why?"

"Do you remember the summer . . . ? No, you wouldn't. You were too little." When she leans to fiddle with the radio, her hair drapes her face in waves.

I think again how pretty she is. She moves slowly now. When she's sitting down and wants something, she always asks, "Would you mind, as long as you're up?"

Of course, we wait on her hand and foot.

"Something happened the summer I turned twelve. I . . . I'm not sure what. I stayed locked in the bedroom by myself most of the time. In fact, I didn't speak to anybody for two months. Finally, Mama took me to Highlands. We stayed there until I got well."

"You didn't talk to anybody for two whole months?"

"Weird, huh?"

"I'll say." I tried to imagine what that would be like, to sit in your room and not say a word. Everybody else would be swimming or playing tennis or at camp, and there you'd be, by yourself in that room, missing it all.

"Boy, I'll bet you were glad it was summer or you'd have been held back for being absent from school so much."

"Yeah." She turns on the blinker, picks up speed to pass a log truck. When she tosses her hair away from her face, she glances at me. "They're afraid I'll get sick again."

"Are you?"

"What?"

"Afraid it'll happen again?"

"Not as much as they are. It feels now like it happened to somebody else."

We both are quiet. Gravel sprinkles the underside of the car. *Ping, ping, ping.* We've hit the construction on I-16. Outside I see green sprigs on the limbs of the sweet gum trees. Tiny islands of greens and pale yellows break through the sparse bare underbrush along the embankment.

Finally, Mary Jo smiles. "You'll look pretty in that bridesmaid's dress with the empire waist. It's your color, should bring out the blue in your eyes."

I catch her hand and press it hard against my cheek. I don't tell her about the big explosions there might be before the wedding and how after that, there might not be a wedding.

Mama pushes her sunglasses up from where they've slid down on the bridge of her nose. Every visit to see Miss Lawson is like reading the same chapter over and over in a book. Without realizing it, Mama lapses into her female static voice. She keeps saying things like, " Mary Jo's too young to even think of trying to raise a child and I certainly don't relish the prospect of taking that responsibility on myself . . . Maybe one day having a baby without being married won't make a difference, but in this day and age, it does. Selfish as this might sound, my main concern is for my child."

I wonder, as I listen to her reasons, who she keeps repeating them for—Miss Lawson or herself?

To Mary Jo, Mama talks about how "giving a baby to someone who will love and cherish and provide it with all the things a child needs is the most unselfish thing an individual can ever be blessed in having the opportunity to do."

Whew, I always think after she's said a mouthful like that.

Outside the car window, the trees and scrubs and grass are a crazy green. Spring is bursting everywhere. Mama's pansies look like polka dots dancing down each side of the front walk. Ivy laces up the chimney in a tangle of mixed greens, so dark it looks almost black in places.

In her last session, Miss Lawson explained about something called open adoption. This is where the mother can stay in contact with the baby after she gives it away. Mama latched onto that idea.

"I know in my heart that if you do decide on adoption, at some point, that child will be back in our lives. If I didn't believe that, why, I couldn't let it out of my sight for one minute. But the decision is yours and you know, honey, we'll support whatever you do."

As we pull into the parking lot of the counseling center, Mama turns and inspects me.

"I wish you hadn't worn that shirt, Ashley," she says. "Tie your lace before you trip on it," she adds.

I think of how I've never heard the words *selfish* and *unselfish* used so many times before in my life.

I slam the door of the car, leave my shoelaces dangling.

Some nights are so dark you can't see your hand in front of your face, but the night we take Mary Jo to the hospital, the moon has lit up the sky like there's a light bulb on overhead. The smell of smoke lingers in the air, the way it does when someone lights a fire in their fireplace. The nights are still chilly but beneath the azalea bushes, a faint shade of lavender tells us the verbena will soon be a purple ruffle.

In the thin darkness, Mama tails me across the driveway, her hand under Mary Jo's arm to steady her. Mary Jo has trouble walking and is bent over, her arms cradling her stomach. Beth carries an overnight bag in one hand, the car keys in the other. Of all things, Daddy is in Atlanta following a lead on a story for the paper. When Mama lets go of Mary Jo, she takes the keys from Beth and slides behind the wheel. "Nervous as I am, I'm still a better driver than you," she tells Beth.

Mary Jo hands me the book of names she was studying when the pains started. She climbs into the back seat and leans back with a groan. A picture of a baby smiling up at me from the front cover of the book reminds me of the day Mary Jo came home and told us she was giving up the baby for adoption.

She'd sat down with a groan then, too. Pulling a pillow behind her, she smoothed her jumper down very carefully in front, like getting the creases out was all she had to think about.

"Mama," she said quietly. "I've decided the only thing to do is what you and Beth want." When she said this, she didn't cry like

I'd have expected her to. In fact, she didn't do anything but sit, smoothing the cloth over that big mound of stomach. Nobody else said anything either. The television was on but turned down so we could barely hear it.

I'd heard Mary Jo up the night before. I guessed she'd been thinking. When I heard what she said, I started thinking, too, thinking there wouldn't be a baby at our house for me to rock after all.

In the backseat, Mary Jo keeps groaning and rubbing big circles on her stomach while Beth keeps track of the contractions—how fast they're coming, how long they last. I do my best not to turn around and look over the seat at Mary Jo, but it's hard. She moans steady as the pains come closer together.

"It hurts so bad," I hear her say to Beth.

Mama yells over her shoulder, saying things to try and make Mary Jo feel better. "Don't worry, honey. You'll be fine. We've got plenty of time. Try and relax. Breathe deep."

When the pains are five minutes apart and we still have six miles to go, Mama shifts into her female static voice. "If Cliff Elkins is sitting someplace in the dark in that patrol car of his, waiting to catch somebody speeding, why he can put me in the jail. I'm getting you to the hospital!"

If they'd been paying attention, they probably wouldn't have let me in the delivery room, but with so much going on, I wind up perched on a stool in a corner beside the door with the book of names in my hand. Mama and Beth stand on either side of Mary Jo, cheering her on—her support system, Mama says. I try to make myself little so nobody will notice I'm there.

Mary Jo lies on the delivery table, crying and moving about like she's trying to get comfortable. A doctor strides into the room, smiling, saying cheery things mainly to Mary Jo. He tells her how all this will soon be over. He wears a bright green outfit that covers all of him, even his head. Another person, in clothes to match the doctor's, a nurse maybe, moves back and forth around the table. She reaches between Mama and Beth to feel Mary Jo's stomach. A big lamp lights everybody from behind with a light as strong as the sun. None of what's going on seems real. It's like we're in a television program with all of us playing different parts.

Mama murmurs to Mary Jo while we wait for the medicine they've given her to work. Beth pats Mary Jo's hand. She keeps taking long, deep breaths through her mouth.

All of a sudden, there's a shuffle of feet, everybody is moving fast. "Here we go," says the doctor, and he scoots his stool up to the end of the table. I stretch my neck to see what's going on, but my view is blocked by Mary Jo's leg. I lean back against the wall and I clutch the book of names to my chest for dear life.

Mary Jo moans one time, long and drawn out. It's so awful, I wish for a minute I'd stayed outside. The skin over her knuckles where she grips the side rails looks pasty in the brilliant light. Then she's quiet, like she's fallen asleep that fast.

The doctor and nurse are busy murmuring and passing instruments back and forth between them. The doctor stands quickly. "Here she is," he says, proudly holding up the baby.

Up to now, I haven't paid much attention to Mama. I glance over at her and when I see her face, I wish the book of names was in her hands instead of mine. She needs something to hold on to. Her face is the chalky shade of Mary Jo's knuckles as she gripped the side rails, pushing down.

The doctor leans toward Mama with the baby in his arms. She places both hands over her mouth and stifles a cry as she stares straight into the baby's tiny red face. A sound tears from her throat. I watch her and feel a catch in my own throat. Suddenly Mama bursts into tears. The nurse starts around the table toward her, but the doctor motions her back.

I don't know what's going on in Mama's mind as she stands there so still and small and crying so hard. What I do know is that she hadn't planned on this.

"What I'm thinking of is my child," I'd heard her say a hundred times to Miss Larson. Now, it's like there's someone else to think of. The baby isn't just Mary Jo's anymore. She's a part of us all.

This is our flesh and blood, I can almost hear Mama thinking. *These are our genes in this baby girl we won't be taking home with us. This baby of ours that will be going to somebody else's house, for them to get up in the middle of the night when she cries for her bottle. Other people will walk the floor with her when she's colicky and sick. Another grandmother will hold her and smile while somebody takes a picture of her wearing lacy white socks and patent leather shoes at Easter.*

I finger the book of names I'm holding in my lap. I can hear Mama saying the words to herself and an empty feeling opens up inside of me. Next time when we're in the car with the rain pouring down, will we feel wrapped in that soft cocoon, or will there be a hole where the rain comes in and that warm safe feeling leaks out?

A heavy throbbing weighs down my chest. I look at everybody, but they all look different. Next to giving up Mary Jo's baby, the things that seemed important before don't matter so much now. Beth and Kevin will get married and everybody in the wedding can be purple with orange polka dots and nobody will care. The reception can be in the back room of Manny's Deli on Delaney Street, the punch served in paper cups as far as we're concerned. It's like all of a sudden, *A Southern Belle Primer* is a joke that everybody gets sooner or later.

The baby makes a soft mewing sound like a kitten. I see Mama's back stiffen. Slowly, she turns. The nurse bundles the baby in a blanket and heads for the door. When she gets even with Mama, she stops. She pushes the blanket aside. Mama stands, gazing down.

"She's beautiful," the nurse says.

"Just perfect, " Mama answers. Tentatively, she reaches over, touches the tiny hand that lies balled into a fist against the baby's cheek. She studies the face like she's trying to memorize it in her mind. Finally she looks at Mary Jo, quiet and still on the delivery table. She glances at Beth, then at me.

"She definitely takes after her mother's side of the family," she says and manages a thin smile.

My fingers hurt from pressing down so hard on the book. I loosen my grip, flip open the cover.

While I sat, watching it all, I'd shredded a page of names, the ones beginning with "D." I see the name *Daisy* in the top corner with the "y" torn in half. I say the word aloud and it slides like a spoonful of Jell-O across my tongue. Suddenly, I realize that the only thing Mary Jo didn't do that Miss Lawson suggested was give the baby a name.

A CHILLY OCTOBER
AFTERNOON

ONE DAY IN late July, I get four postcards from Annie. After the first, I know there is another, then another, because at the bottom of each she writes, *See next.*

She tells me that she's in Perth, Australia, teaching at the university there. The back of the first card pictures a dense grove of eucalyptus, the coin-shaped leaves on the trees coated a dust-colored silver that makes them look iridescent against the arid brown landscape. In the distance, I see a gathering of sheep slant toward me from the side of a gently curving plain. She asks if I'd like her to ship me some lamb's wool. It's dreadfully inexpensive, she says. She's been there for a month and encloses her new address. At the end of the last card, the one I almost miss because it's caught between my electricity bill and an advertisement for a combination washer-dryer from Maytag, she's written in tiny letters I can scarcely read, "*I hate mutton.*"

I chuckle and understand how much of what Annie tells me isn't written on the cards. She's feeling terribly alone in that dustbowl of lamb chops and weeping pines. Could I write to her until she feels a connection with someone or something there? She needs to know that she's connected somewhere.

Although I will answer Annie's cards, I hesitate, take time to think of what I'll say. If I'm not careful, my resentments at her will flair.

I still can't look at a can of sardines without shuddering when I think of the rancid smelling oil she poured into the trash can in our dorm room almost twenty-five years ago. "Yes, I know," she agreed when I came through the doorway holding my nose. "I guess that wasn't such a smart thing to do." After that, she flushed the oil down the commode for a while until she forgot again, and the smell of stale fish lingered. Annie never seemed to comprehend that if I didn't like sardines, neither would I like the ripe heavy smell of the oil in which they were packed—her brilliance once again eroded by the missing link in her logic.

Or did I misread her even then? Was it simply naiveté that I mistook for something more complicated? Unlike her, I'd been schooled in a home where nothing could be taken at face value. But, the humorous approach—my personal Band-Aid for life's numerous maladies—played well off her simple view of reality.

I think of our senior year, the picnic at Cedar Lake and the outrageous price she paid for fresh tomatoes for the salad.

"Well, I certainly hope you got the ones with the gold centers?" I asked factiously.

"No, you wanted the ones with the gold centers?" she replied, her face a study in innocence.

As I think back, there were other things I resented. There was the way her skirt, a butter yellow color, cupped her rear in a smooth unwrinkled line when she cocked her hip to one side; and how she never lost any of the charms off her bracelet, although she wore it even in the shower.

But most of all, I resent the afternoon love affair she had with my father.

I tilt the cards back and forth now as if I am about to shuffle them. I have to ask myself if I, who shudders at the thought of sardines, am honestly sorry that Annie-in-some-faraway-land is greeted every day by the warm smell of freshly slaughtered sheep.

Since Dad died, I hear from Annie infrequently. When he was alive, it was more often. I was groomed to act as her conduit. "You say your father is . . . ?" she'd start to ask, and I'd fill in the blanks for her.

As I feel the sharp edge of the cards bite into my skin, I think of that afternoon so many years before. I sat perched on a hassock facing my mother, our knees touching and our heads bent close, stringing together the beads of Annie's broken necklace. I lined the brightly colored pieces, round and smooth as creek pebbles, across the flat of my hand in the intricate pattern to match those few left hanging from the string. My mother took each bead from my palm and held it as if she were threading a needle—one green, two reds, a black, three blues—sliding the slender thread into the hole in one end and out the other in her graceful way, like stitching together the ruffled sleeve of a blouse.

When she looked up and saw Annie and my father standing in the doorway, she clasped her hands, cupping the beads together. The pattern of the necklace dissolved in a jumble. The beads slipped through her fingers and scattered across the floor as if she were sprinkling the carpet in a shower of broken rainbow.

Outside in the foyer, the grandfather clock, which my father wound faithfully every Saturday morning, had stopped. If it had been working, it would have chimed the hours. One, two, three, four, five, six. He and Annie had left before noon for Sullivan's pecan orchard behind our house. Annie had never seen a pecan-picker-upper like the one Dad had found the week before at TruValue. He'd demonstrate how easily the slender rod with the cup on the end scooped up the nuts. No bending, no stooping, he explained, his black hair with the random streaks of gray curling back from his long forehead in crisp even waves. Bundled warmly in sweaters and jackets against the first cold snap of the year, he and Annie went down the steps together, laughing, their breath exploding in powdery puffs of brisk air.

It was October. Slick brown needles from the four towering loblollies at the corners of the yard carpeted our front lawn. A chilled breeze stripped the live oaks in flurries, leaving heaps of colored leaves to decorate the eaves of the house in subtle shades of rust and gold. With its strength ebbing, the wind stole through the slits in the windows to stir the tassels on the shades.

Annie and I had graduated in June. She'd decided to go on to graduate school at Emory in Atlanta. She'd come to see me one more time before the holidays. On the first night of her visit she'd snagged her necklace on a button while undressing and the necklace broke, spilling beads in all directions.

It's the only one I own," she reminded me while the two of us crawled across the floor searching for the last bead, a purple one we found hidden beneath a corner bedpost.

"And it goes with everything," I finished for her, picturing how she wore it with her lemon-colored sweater even though it clashed with the buttons at the neck.

The next morning, thinking that she and Dad wouldn't be long in the orchard, I gathered the loose beads and coarse thread and settled on the hassock to begin restringing the necklace—a surprise for when she returned. At her desk in a corner of the room, my mother watched the back door through which Annie and Dad had disappeared. After a long while of sitting with her hands folded loosely in her lap, she slid her work into a top drawer. "Pull your stool up here in this good light," she said, coming to sit in the wing-back chair beside the lamp. "I'll help you."

Before threading a bead on the string, she'd examine it, holding it up to watch the shimmering colors spin and play in the light. From the second she took the beads into her hands, she seemed captivated by their beauty.

"I can't imagine why I've never noticed this before. It's a lovely necklace. So many different colors. It must go with everything."

I smiled, assured her that yes, Annie thought so, too.

My mother left her chair for short periods that blustery afternoon and I did the same—for trips to the bathroom, to stretch our legs, to answer an occasional ringing of the phone. Yet as time passed and Annie and my father didn't return, we seemed drawn back to our places in front of the fireplace, back to the broken necklace.

Our progress was slow. The pattern was complicated. A tiny gold disc fitted snugly between each bead. Some of the beads were solid in color, while others were mingled and smoky. The discs were so small, they kept sliding back and forth, slipping through our fingers. Several times we had to begin again, restringing what had already been done.

Eventually, Mother glanced more and more at the picture of my father on the end table beside her chair. She looked at it with a hard, steady gaze, a look I'd seen before when the two of them had quarreled. The photo was an old one that through the years had become something of a family joke. It showed Dad as a young man in the Navy, in dress whites with his fist propped dramatically on his chin, like a touched-up glamour photo in some movie magazine.

While the long autumn afternoon took its first firm step toward winter and an early dusk crept darkly along the fence hedge, we sat, straining for a sound from outside—boots scraping against cold concrete, laughter, a cry. Perhaps one of them had fallen. *There you see, that explains* . . . Keeping my eyes on our hands, I tried to keep my mind on our busywork. Neither of us spoke of Dad and Annie's lengthy absence, although it became as tangible as the fragile pieces of necklace we held between us.

I heard the slap of the screen door first, then the rustle of footsteps in the foyer. When Annie and my father appeared in the doorway, my hands stopped as if on their own and fell into my lap.

I'd never thought of Annie as especially pretty. Her face seemed something unfinished, a bit more flesh along the cheekbones, the tilt of an eyebrow. Her skin was pale, her hair and eyebrows the faded color of sun-bleached hay as if in the making of her, the tint had somehow been omitted. But when she walked into the room, she looked as lovely as a painting. Her huge brown eyes with their permanent hint of sadness were made even larger by the loose easy waves that framed her face. In a splash of lamplight from the hallway, her chin had lost its sharpness. Her lips held a new fullness that was enhanced by the high glow in her cheeks. Only when I glanced at my father did I realize that this new softness in Annie had little to do with the light.

The fine lines around his mouth had disappeared. His face was mellow, with a gentleness that I recognized from the old photograph and knew must be left over from sometime in his youth. And like Annie, his face was flushed, too, a dark ruddy tan against the stark white of his clergy's collar.

Through the long afternoon, Mother, in whom patience wasn't ordinarily much at home anyway, had ruffled her fingers through her hair again and again. As she stood and watched them now, a rumpled look lingered about her that made me want to reach up and tidy the loose strands that crept down her neck. I suddenly wanted to smooth the wrinkled collar of her sweater. Although she stood still as a carved statue, at her temple a slender blue vein pulsed and throbbed as her heartbeat quickened in her breast. I felt the hollow, gray knot that had built inside me all the afternoon. It sat in my stomach as heavy as a stone. But for me, it was a familiar feeling. It was always there when I couldn't predict what Mother was about to do next.

While I sat, still and tense, searching as I did in these moments for something to say, I thought of my father and Annie as they had sat in front of the fireplace together last evening.

"You put the kindling in first," he'd explained to her. "'Then crisscross the logs on top."

Annie had listened intently, then struggled with the heavy pieces of wood as if she'd never had to think of how a fire was lit before. In that huge house in the north Georgia foothills where there were servants to stoke the fire, Annie's elderly parents had discouraged anything that might take their brilliant daughter away from her studies. The touch of melancholy that clung with near permanence to her face disappeared only when there was a book in her hands or, as it did then, in the light from the bristling fire with my father at her side.

Now, Annie shrugged out of her jacket. With a smile, she turned and took the pecan-picker from my father. But when she looked at Mother and me, Annie paused. Her smile faded. My father hesitated as well. With his arm half out of his jacket, he sent a side-glance toward my mother.

Although I didn't know what was about to happen, I knew there were times when Mother attacked Dad almost without provocation. She'd lash out at him with bitter sarcasm, accusations or crudely veiled innuendoes. When this occurred, I'd watch him close in on himself. He'd bury his natural gentleness beneath a detachment so impenetrable that she was sealed away from him. I never understood what made their marriage so difficult. My childhood was spent watching them struggle, forever thinking that if I could say something funny enough, laughter would be the glue that would keep them sealed together.

Mother looked down at her clutched hands, at the scarlet bead she held there. Slowly, she turned her hands back and forth as she'd done earlier in the afternoon, watching the light dance across the brilliant colors. I could read the calculation in her face as she examined this bead, the one that peeked like a tiny searchlight between her fingertips. She seemed to think something would be revealed to her by the roundness of its shape or the cold feel of the glass as it lay flat against her flesh. Annie wasn't one of those women with slack mouths of whom Mother could say behind the back of her hand, "She's known for her looseness, you know." I could tell that Mother, who thought she read people well, didn't quite know what to make of Annie.

Finally she dropped the loose bead in my lap. Then she lifted the string and meticulously threaded onto it a bead the polished green color of mint jelly. Without looking up, she held out her hand for another.

Dad, with the familiar lines creasing his mouth again and the flush receding from his face, slid out of the sturdy hunting jacket.

Glancing once more at Mother, he moved heavily into the foyer. He took the key from atop the clock and opened its beveled glass door. He placed the key in the tiny hole in front and turned until it was tight. From beside the fireplace, I watched him tap the edge of the pendulum with the tip of his finger to send it swinging back and forth. With that he moved the hands to set time in place and gently closed the door.

Meanwhile, Annie had come to stand beside the fireplace. Perhaps in an attempt to overcome the tense quiet in the room, she clapped her hands together briskly. The sharp sound broke through the silence with a loud *Crack! Crack!* She looked around frantically as if she were about to be reprimanded for making a racket on a solemn Sunday afternoon in the parlor where children were seen and not heard.

Dad, who'd made his way back through the doorway, didn't appear to notice. He kept his head down and stopped at the newspaper that lay opened on a table beside the couch. While he stood, reading the day's headlines, my glance went from him to the man in the photograph at my mother's elbow. The light from the foyer was brighter now that dusk had passed and new darkness had arrived. Lit from behind by this sharp, true glow, his profile held the same fine sensual lines as the one in the picture. In both there was the proud arch of the chin, the slight hump at the bridge of his otherwise sleekly chiseled nose.

While I studied these two images of my father, I thought of my junior year in college, when the two semesters of adoration for an especially exacting English professor had culminated in a single afternoon of exquisite lovemaking on the overstuffed couch in his office. I had cherished the friction burns on my elbows from the sofa's rough fabric that took weeks to disappear.

As I listened to the crackle of logs in the fireplace, the faint *whish* of wind at the window, I could have told Mother what to make of Annie. She'd fallen in love with my father. Frankly, I wondered what had taken her so long.

Holding up a bead that looked like the eye of a tiger, I winked at her. "Here's looking at ya, kid."

Smiling, she sank beside me on the hassock, reached for a bead, a clear fiery blue. She held it against her cheek. Her hands, sharply outlined by the firelight, seemed to end in hollow shadows laid like faded bruises along the delicate undersides of her wrists. The glow was gone from her face, the bead's blue reflection that lay muted against her cheek was her only color now.

I thought at that moment that if someone had dropped by for a visit, we'd have turned to them and smiled. "My, how delighted we are to see you. Won't you come in?" Yet the knot in my stomach was still there as my mother selected a bead and slowly threaded it through the string as though the next color to choose was her only concern.

In the hallway, I heard the grandfather clock chime the hour. For all the clock knew, the things that happened while it was stopped might never have occurred at all.

Leaning the postcards from Annie side by side against the table lamp on my mother's desk, I admire the vivid collage of colors. On the one nearest the light, a baby koala hangs suspended from the scaly limb of a tree. With enormous black eyes, it peers suspiciously into the camera.

I'll write that I'd like the lamb's wool Annie offered to send. Mother spends most of her time in bed now since her fractured hip. They say lamb's wool is soft on the skin.

I'll tell Annie how I read to Mother, mostly the Bible. She laughs when I remind her of how it doesn't hurt either of us to hear it. Recently, she's grown attached to a columnist in *The Constitution*. "My kind of humor," she says with a chuckle.

I stack the cards into a neat pile, then slide them into the top drawer of the desk. Lately, when I read to my mother, I have trouble keeping track of where I've stopped. I won't tell Annie, but the cards will make perfect bookmarks to keep me from losing my place.

CLOWNS

"LUTHER IS ON a prison farm in Jester," my sister Jo tells me over the phone late into the night, her voice bleary with wine. "Ramos and I went to see him before he left." She hesitates. I see her, squinting, circling the tip of the cigarette with a lighter. It catches, glows brilliantly. I hear her dry, brittle cough. Reaching wearily for a pillow, I lift my head, prop the pillow beneath it, sink back into the softness.

"I can't begin to know how you must feel," I tell her. This is true. Unlike her son Luther, my children are insulated in respectability. Daddy chose a perfect father for them. But I don't tell her this.

I sent her a poem once, clipped from an issue of *Ladies Home Journal*. It was sandwiched between a story of a grandmother whose rheumatism left her in peace after a trip to Lourdes and a Bisquick recipe for oyster bisque. A sentimental poem and quite unrealistic, it went something like this:

> *As sisters we discovered life*
> *as one for a time*
> *Knowing always at the end of the lane*
> *stood the open gate . . .*

Jo thought it was an enchanting poem. I'd sent her my only copy. I wish now that I'd kept one for myself since I've forgotten the best parts of it.

We were mistaken for twins so often we began to parrot our mother's words. *No! No! Not twins. Sixteen months apart lacking one day.*

If we're not twins, why do we have to wear look-alike dresses? we cried. The dresses were ruffled at the neck and ankles, plumpish in teal blue pinafores the shade of our eyes. *Your father wants you to. You'll do it for Daddy, won't you?*

I kicked Jo on the shin, leaving a shadowy bruise. *See, we're not twins. I don't have a bruise*, I said, extending an unblemished calf.

If I'd known, I could have waited. It was the same spot on Jo's leg where the scar was later.

The night after I'd bruised her leg, an owl or something like an owl hooted in the night. Frightened, I curled beneath the patchwork quilt and searched for Jo's hand across our wide double bed.

Jo hiccups softly and says, "They told me prisoners are processed, whatever that means, before they're locked up. They finished with Luther before we could get there. Ramos and I can handle not seeing him, Laney, but I'm not sure Luther can handle not seeing us."

I gaze out the window into the darkness. So many phone calls in the night, the slurring more pronounced with the lateness of the hour.

One Christmas, Mother sent the three of us—Daddy, Jo and me—to search for a tree. We marched single file, dodging tree stumps and crumpled barbed wire fences, laughing when Daddy flopped like a limp-limbed Mortimer Snerd in our path. We discovered the tree deep in a thick stand of pines. It was a Loblolly, gigantic and grand, with spreading branches to fill the space in front of the window where the couch sat, the carpet rich beneath it, hidden away from the brilliant sunlight all summer.

Daddy cleared his throat, a raspy file grating across serrated metal. "Okay, girls, straighten up. Your mother considers this finding a Christmas tree serious business." He sank the axe blade into the crisp bark, chopping away.

But I wanted to play. Laughing, I pushed Jo; she tripped and tumbled against Daddy's shoulder. The axe glanced off the knobby bark of the tree and the blade bounced, slicing into the soft flesh on the back of her leg. I stared, frozen, as blood welled frothy over the lips of the wound.

"Quick, Laney!" Daddy shouted. "Throw your sweater to me." He twisted the sweater around and around the gaping cut. Lifting Jo onto his back, he ran, jogging as if playing a game of piggyback except for the panic and the busy pattern of red mingling with the ripply blues and greens of my sweater. He struggled through dog fennel and blackberry bushes, catching the brambles with his shoulders and pushing them roughly away. Behind him, the broken limbs whipped back, tangling in my curls like jumbled pick-up sticks. Daddy stopped only once to rest.

"Run, Laney! Have your mother call Dr. Fletcher and tell him we're on our way."

My heart beat so fast. Jo's head had fallen limply against Daddy's neck. But for one keen, high scream, she hadn't made a sound.

I moisten my lips now as I remember, and the ripe, bitter taste of dog fennel seems to linger still on my tongue.

Jo, home for the first time from Georgia Southern, squealed when Daddy held my high school yearbook open for her to see. "Oh, Laney, you got 'Most Humorous' in your senior class, too!" I tilted my head in appropriate modesty and covered my mouth with my hands to stifle a silly giggle.

"I ask for brains and what do I get? Clowns!" Daddy said, shuddering in mock horror.

"Comedians!" Jo and I cried as one. She crossed her eyes and minced pigeon-toed across the room toward me. I spread two fingers in a wide "V" and pretended to plunge them into her eyes as we slid into a Curly and Moe pantomime, *nyuk, nyuking* at each other.

At supper Daddy toasted the two of us with great ceremony, bowing solemnly first to Jo, then to me.

Under the Christmas tree that year, Jo and I found identical orange horses with blue saddles tucked far back into the piney fragrance. They were splendid horses, with delicate threads for bridles and hooves circled in stripes of slender ebony, the kind of horses that prance into circus arenas with clowns clinging to their back.

"We called his parole officer ourselves. He stole our MasterCard. We had to do it."

What am I supposed to do, ease your conscience?

"You do what you have to do," I say gingerly, lamely, staring at the watermark from the leaky roof on the ceiling above my head.

When Jo came home from Connecticut for the first time with Luther, her tawny Spaniard, my blue-eyed Harrison napped beside him in the parlor, away from our chatter.

"A Cuban from New York City and Catholic at that! Never!" Daddy had shouted at her. "Not in this family!" He then pleaded, "I'll give you anything, Johanna. You want a car? I'll give you a car."

"No, Daddy. I want you to walk me down the aisle."

I glance at the clock on my bedside table, knowing that when the alarm rings at dawn, I'll struggle sluggish and gray into the morning.

* * *

The chapel was small. A priest came from St. Augustine for confessions on Saturday nights and again for mass on Sundays. Jo's hair cupped each ear like a gravy ladle; a pageboy, it was called. Under the long Victorian gown, her limp was barely discernible to anyone who didn't know it was there.

"I'll never cause you such pain, Daddy," I promised.

I didn't, either. My little Harrison grew up in the stone house next door where salvia and dusty miller skirt the cement walk leading to the front door.

I ease from the bed and with the tip of my toe, nudge closed the half-open door of my closet. A moonbeam catches, shimmering sickle-thin on a satin robe inside.

A classmate disappeared into the deepest part of the lake before we were old enough to know that death meant forever. To us, Arlene was simply away on a visit to her grandmother's in Jacksonville. Tomorrow she'd be back home, splashing about in mud puddles wearing her red rubber boots.

"Laney, Ramos had an affair. But it's over now and things are fine, better for it actually."

If it's not working, Jo, you don't have to defend him. You don't have to pretend. Daddy's no longer here to know, I want to say.

Tip-toeing into the dim lit room, we stared at Grandmother Emerson, still and white as porcelain under the draped canopy, and searched for the flicker from those eyelids rimmed in heavy shadow. Jo leaned close, looked intently at a tuft of gray stubble in one of the brown moles peppering Grandmother's chin. Tentatively, she touched the tiny blemish that marred her own slender neck. "If I ever get like that," she whispered, "promise you'll pluck my chin hairs for me."

* * *

Drowsy now, I feel the sand beneath my eyelids. I picture high-spirited Luther and then my dependable, predictable Harrison, such an easy child and so like his father. Not a heartache in his bones.

"You ripped it, Jo," I yelled, holding up the taffy-colored blouse for her to see.

"I didn't," she yelled back. "It was ripped already, before I borrowed it."

Another time, I ignored her for days because of a fight over a tartan skirt, after first hurling her bottle of Evening In Paris against the wall on her side of the room. "See if I pluck your chin hairs for you when you're dying and paralyzed and can't move your limbs," I screamed as she dashed out the door wearing my turquoise cardigan buttoned down the back.

When Daddy died, we learned that death isn't as we'd thought at all. It's silent and empty—a thickening in our throats that blocks the pain and keeps it bottled up inside.

"Rachael was in an accident and I had to reach him. At the very moment our daughter needed him, he was with that woman."

Fringes of pale daylight edge my windowsill. I listen to the sound of her weeping, wait for it to stop. I don't tell her of my lover who speaks with a stilted British accent and excites me as my Wasp has never done; how I clutch at handfuls of wiry black hair while he buries himself deep inside me, draws a cry, then leaves me sated and drowsy.

At her wedding, I walked down the aisle with spit curls pressed like copper coins against my cheeks, a rhinestone stitched into each blossom on the dress she'd chosen for me to wear.

"Is it my fault, Laney?" she asks now through little girl sobs.

I gaze down the length of the bed at my legs, their tan dark against the teal blue bedspread. What am I to say? How do I know?

Her legs were more shapely than mine, softly rounded and tapering, while mine were merely sturdy and substantial. She wore black and white saddle oxfords and stretched bobby sox that set off her ankles nicely.

When I ran past Daddy and Jo through the pines, the blood spilled down and settled in the cuff of Daddy's trousers where it lay clotted, draping over like a thick purple tongue. I weighed five pounds less than Jo and would have been so much easier for him to carry on his back.

"Am I to blame?" she asks again. My chest aches at the heartbreak in her voice. For once, she needs more than my listening ear.

"Sometimes no one's to blame."

The watermark over my bed is shaped like a map of the island where my lover was born. The mark on the ceiling grows larger and the salvia more brilliant when the rains begin in June.

THE FLOWER PIT

IN LATE EVENING, when dusk hovered in the violet remains of daylight, he discovered the body of his gypsy wife, Faith. The body lay sprawled in the flower pit, the cave-like winter haven for succulent plants located in the backyard. You can say this for him—he gave her a decent burial even after he found the drifter's body beside her in the pit. After all, she had made a tire swing in the backyard for his children, the same backyard where chance had placed her the summer before.

Everyone knew something dreadful was bound to happen from the second the gypsy woman with her jaunty step and flashing eyes entered their lives. With their bewitching smiles, gypsies were known for stealing the time from clocks, heat from the sun and a wise man's reason. Everyone knew this except him, that is. He didn't see Faith like that. What he saw that hot summer day she appeared, with her gay skirts billowing and her gold bracelets clinking like castanets, was hope. Hope that here, finally, was someone to dispel the grief that had arrowed itself into his soul when his first wife, Lydia, had died. As he watched Faith dance across his backyard and listened to her magical gypsy laughter, desire stirred in him like flurries of spooked quail rising in sheets of wind along the fence line.

* * *

It happened in a part of the country with a bold history of grandeur and plenty in the meager time that came after that august past. Gone were the white columns, demitasse spoons, and Charlotte Russe. Now fatback and grits, leaking roofs and rugged labor strangled the sharecropper's spirit. It trampled his pride and left him mean and stingy with a need to get back at someone.

Only the flowers spoke of the splendor left from that fine and prosperous era. Waxed begonias, their stiff verdigris leaves encircling white-scented blossoms, the beguiling rex, the hairy-jointed leaves sprouting reds and greens and golds, the fruity geraniums that blanketed the sleeping porch with lemon and pineapple smells.

The winding driveways edged in purple verbena and dogwoods had disappeared. The flowers were no longer arrayed in elegant gardens with formal borders and fine arbors, but their blossoms were no less splendid now in coffee cans lining rickety porch steps. Traveling past on the washboard roads, if you didn't look quickly you'd miss the twisted Jasmine. But once you'd slowed and gazed a moment at the hillside, you'd spot the tiny white blossoms twinkling against the sagging foundations of burned houses and tumbled-down chimneys.

The flower pit, his last gift to Lydia before she died, was a basement of sorts that sat apart from the house. Carved six feet below ground, the cellar-like room stretched twelve feet wide with steps angled down from one corner to the sawdust floor below. A heavy trap door of latticed four by fours allowed stripes of meager sunlight to nurture the plants. Bricks stationed around the top sealed leaks and prevented snakes and small animals from hibernating inside when the cold set in. Rattlesnakes, common in the area and always a threat, especially loved the pit's dark warmth.

The pit had sounded simple in the planning, but problems popped up right away when he began the actual building of it. Lydia had wanted it above the waterline, so he'd dug it on a rise on the south side of the yard that left nothing to break the force of the Nor'easters roaring through. Wind kept ripping away the canopy top he'd installed that rolled back on fair weather days and let in the sun. The heavy wooden door he used to replace the flimsy canvas stayed in place but was difficult for Lydia to lift. Once the pole that propped the door ajar had slipped and the door slammed shut, trapping two-year-old James inside. So the children's father had attached a sturdy lock on the outside of the door and they were forbidden from playing in that corner of the yard again.

Finally the day arrived when he knew he either had to marry Faith or turn her away. And it was too late to turn her away. He'd been without anchor and she rekindled his life with purpose.

They were married one day in May and together they cherished the loamy soil and abundant flowers. He loved nothing more than the smell of earth recently turned by the plow's edge, and she, to bring the fertile potting soil to her lips, tasting its richness, testing the grainy texture against her tongue. Unlike fine-boned and delicate Lydia, Faith with her strong back and firm muscles had no trouble lifting and lowering the cumbersome flower pit door.

But those who'd predicted doom knew better than he did about the wild spirit that ruled her. They waited and watched while she taught his children the magic of the stars, how to catch tadpoles in the swift creek and lightning bugs in the night sky. She taught James to tie his shoes and three-year-old Amanda to brush her teeth until they dazzled. While Lydia had served lace cornbread and teacakes for supper, Faith threw everything into one big pot. She stirred the stewed rabbits and fried squirrels, day-old rice, black-eyed peas and steamed okra together into a delicious Mulligan Stew the children relished.

But sure enough, the day came when the wildness Faith struggled to tame finally broke free.

The children wondered when she wasn't in the kitchen at supper. By the time their father returned from the fields, they'd begun to cry. Shushing them, he searched for her, calling her name in the dwindling light. Finally he found her nestled beside the drifter at the bottom of the pit.

They were still there when the sheriff arrived, summoned the next morning at dawn. The poison and their struggle to escape had not been kind to their bodies; the sheriff shuddered and turned away. He was a good sheriff, intent on doing his job well, and so he set about attending to his tasks. Searching the rim of the pit, he found the missing brick where the rattler had slid inside. The sheriff studied the hole and the freshly-turned earth around it for a long time, then gazed silently across the corn field that edged the yard. After a while, he commented on the drought and the thirsty corn stalks with their curling leaves and parched tassels. A man for whom small talk never came easily, he parsed his words, doling them out like one might count the grains in a teaspoonful of sugar. The freshness of the earth around the hole, the accusing angle of the brick and the padlock lying an innocent distance away, he never mentioned at all.

SAM

THE WHEELS ON the folding cot skid as Richard scoots it along in search of the condo number. When the cot tilts in the pebbly street, he scrambles to set it upright and the wire frame slices his thumb, drawing blood. He sucks at the cut. Then he swipes at a line of sweat trickling down his sunburned nose. He's heard that people with blue eyes suffer the most from sun glare. Not so! His eyes are a muddy tan, but his head feels hollowed out like a Halloween pumpkin. Cupping his hands to shade his eyes, he spots 214 again for the third go round. Obviously he's lost.

Suddenly his heart does its funny stutter that Alice calls heart farts. He waits, praying breathlessly. Please God, if there is a You and You're paying attention, don't let this be the Big One. When he feels his heart regain its footing, he sighs and drops to the curb.

Richard had expected his demise to result from old age, not from pushing a stupid bed around in circles. And it's all Alice's fault. If she didn't have this thing about sleeping with him, he wouldn't be out here risking sunstroke and heart failure beneath this vast blue sky so wide and empty it makes his eyes ache.

The two of them have traveled from Asheville to St. Petersburg, sleeping in the same room but in separate beds, of course. This morning they'd arrived at her son Peter's condo complex, where they'd be staying in the guest suite. The only problem is the suite has only one double bed. Peter was nice enough to rent the cot for them. Richard was to wheel it from Peter's condo to the guest suite, but where the hell is it? Richard is the first to admit his thinking isn't as sharp as it used to be, but he could swear Peter had said, "Bear right and you can't miss it."

Sunlight glitters off shiny flecks in the concrete; the heat swallows him in its shimmering vapor. The new complex was carved out of an orange grove where now not a single tree is in sight. His flamingo shirt, fresh and crisp this morning, drapes his neck and shoulders like a soggy towel.

A man with busy eyebrows honks and waves triumphantly as he wheels past in a black Land Rover.

Of course the man and his slick panache remind Richard of his brother Sam. When Sam and Alice were married and before Sam died, Richard had watched his brother pull Alice close and, holding her face in his hands, caress her skin as luscious as a fresh plum. He'd search her blue eyes, studying them as if they were an intricate road map to Paradise.

Now Richard pictures himself in that delectable position—he's always treasured his brother's lush leftovers—but he can't seem to pull it off. Alice has said she has no time for mooning around, and the truth be known, Richard is no match for Sam with his bold swagger and black curl tilted rakishly over one eye, dead or alive.

Even with his brother gone these twelve years now and the bloom wilted from Alice's luminous skin, Richard's touches are tentative and cunningly timed for when she isn't aware—a shadow on the shoulder or the light brush of a palm inside the elbow. "Oops, sorry," he says if she pulls quickly away. If only she didn't think of him as such a loser. He can never answer the question of whether he really is a loser, or if her passion in believing it makes him feel so inept.

Still, he knows he could do a better job of convincing her that he's not. Last night when Alice donned her indoor face of dim lights and pulled blinds, he leaned close to savor her warm buttery smell and chanced a courageous peck on her cheek.

"Believe me when I say I'm not hearing bells," she said mean-spiritedly. Recently he heard her explain him to an acquaintance when he was almost out of earshot but not quite. 'Fog, you know, as in dense and dreary." While she was a little bit Alice when Sam was alive, she's a lot more Alice now. Richard often asks himself why he bothers, but he knows the answer. Even though he suspects she frequently thinks of him as something hard to shake, like a stubborn wad of gum on the bottom of her shoe, he can't fathom life without her. Yet, he must admit, now and again nano-thoughts have flashed across his mind like the blips on his cardiac monitor after his open-heart surgery. What would life be like without Alice? Would I feel as if my heart had been yanked out by the roots like I did when they cracked open my chest and unplugged my arteries?

No matter how hard he tries, words he never intends to utter leap sprightly from his lips. "Did you hear what he said, Alice? D-o-u-b-l-e-b-e-d!" He spelled out the word. "We won't even be touching."

"On the surface, you're a good sport, Richard, but underneath you're a whiner. Now make yourself useful as well as ornamental and hand me that magazine," she ordered with a look that leveled him.

He'd excused her peremptory remark. Even he knows how tempting it is to kick a cowering mongrel. Besides, no one has ever referred to him as "a good sport" before, or for that matter "ornamental" either.

As he watches the Land Rover pull away, a movement on the curb catches his eye. He glances down to see a chameleon scurry down the sloping lawn. The tiny creature dashes across the hot pavement into the shade of an oleander melting from green to the muted gray-brown color of the mulch scattered beneath the bush. It stops and stares back at Richard. From the sudden stillness of its pose, it appears sculpted in weathered tin. As it sits frozen, Richard imagines watching the picture of himself from behind the narrowed eyes.

He knows even without the bed, he gives the appearance of being high strung and ineffectual. With his delicate fine-boned features and his tendency to hyperventilate, he's spent a good portion of his life explaining, *No, actually, I'm not gay.* He understands the confusion. Before his retirement as an English professor, his classroom attire was a silk cravat decorated in paisley print and his lectures were delivered with a swishy flair. It's not his fault that his mannerisms are effeminate and he's never married. Lord knows he's tried. The women he'll have won't have him.

His head throbs now when he thinks of how miserable his life has failed to live up to the brilliant possibilities he'd devised for it. What happened? When did he lose his snap and crackle? He's tried to do the right thing, the honorable thing, and lied only when he's had to. From the beginning he knew that destiny had played a horrible trick on him when it planted him on the chicken farm near Odessa. The sweat that poured down his back felt strange and foreign to his skin. *What on earth am I doing here?* he'd ask himself in dismay. He hated the burning sun that blistered his fair skin, peeling off layer after layer until he felt like a worn eraser nub. Sam, with the merry Huck Finn whistle, saw nothing wrong with living poised at the edge of the desert. Like the rugged desert tortoises that survived for hundreds of years in 140 degrees temperature, Sam thrived in the relentless heat, his copper skin as tough as beef jerky. Meanwhile, Richard felt trapped. He thought only of the unfairness of it. When he gathered eggs in the musty chicken coop, nothing rankled him more than the wasted energy of the cackling Rhode Island Reds in their feeble attempts at flight. Despite their great commotion of flapping wings, they were trapped forever by their inability to fly. To them, the top roost was Mt. Everest. To Richard, it was nothing short of failure.

After the kissing episode last night, Richard jumped out of the path of the latest issue of *Vogue* Alice had flung across the room at him. She'd just pointed out a photograph of a handsome man standing on the deck of a cruise ship. Sam again, always Sam.

Richard had to admit the likeness was uncanny. A much younger Sam with the famous dangling curl. Sam's lock of hair seemed to fall naturally into its sexy, suave curl. But it didn't, Richard wanted to tell Alice. Sam worked at that curl. In the picture, the man's bronze chest matted in springy black hair, is muscled and fit and shouts of everything manly. This youthful, virulent Sam, the one who sits forever on the back porch of Alice's mind, is the one she searches for in magazines, on billboards, on television programs, in movies. She always finds him and when she does, she makes sure that Richard sees him, too.

"Well, the nose is different, and Sam loved speed boats, not cruises." Somehow Richard could never give her the satisfaction of saying, "Why yes, that does resemble Sam."

Late last night, when Alice was in bed, Richard studied the photo again. The nose wasn't different; it was the same as Sam's and that was damned near perfect. So were his chiseled chin, the subtle curve of his lips—plus the fact that Sam, who'd stayed behind with the chickens, had one day discovered barrels and barrels of rich black crude beneath the hen house. So wouldn't anyone have felt second rate to Sam, not just Richard?

Suddenly a lime green Volkswagen Bug with two young women in the front seat sweeps around the corner, followed by a long yellow Hummer. Richard watches wide-eyed. He's never seen anything like the Hummer. Stretching like a boxed set of doublewide Jeeps, it seems to go on forever. It's just the kind of absurd vehicle Sam, with his bold swagger and black curl tilted rakishly over one eye, loved. The petulant young man in the Hummer waves at the girls in the Bug. Then the girl behind the wheel does a double take when she sees Richard and the bed. Giggling, she gives a long shrill blast on the horn. "Nice bed, Pops," yells the girl with purple lips in the passenger seat. "Check out that cool flamingo shirt! Whoo-o-o, who-o-oo, whoo-o-o."

Richard pushes himself up from the curb. For a second he's not sure what to think. He's reminded of the young women he used to teach. Ordinarily, he deemed their loud noise and rowdy nature unnecessary disruptions. But something about the girl with the grape lips urges him to wave back. He likes that she's taken notice of him. The Hummer lumbers away, but the Bug slows almost to a stop. When the girl smiles, Richard smiles back. Suddenly she jerks open her blouse and leans bare-breasted toward him out of the window. "Oh, my goodness," Richard mutters and catches his breath in wonder. In the sunlight the young woman's breasts are luminous and polished, a voluptuous Rubens escaped after centuries of hanging captive on a stuffy museum wall. He is about to turn his eyes demurely away when he stops. No, this young lady is offering him a gift and, by golly, he's going to take it! Breathing in and out, he smiles gamely and a bracing feeling of bravado washes over him. Not only will he accept it, he'll accept it with gratitude. He throws back his shoulders and salutes her with a huge grin.

With cirrus clouds nudging the dazzling blue overhead, he swings his arms back and forth. They feel loose and free at his side. His sunburned skin no longer constricts. The same powerful energy surges through him that years ago propelled him into action in the hot Texas sun. He tosses back his head and slides his thumbs under his collar with a jaunty flip. Funny how a little thing like magnificent breasts can lift one's spirits. Loser? What loser? He's no loser.

Richard waves until the breasts disappear from sight. Chuckling to himself, he ducks and fades back into a shadow box that turns into a tricky dance step. A little madness in the spring is good even for the King!

He's about to swagger away when his eyes light on the bed looming beside him in the street. He glances at the chameleon with its one raised foot and disquieting turn of its head still staring up at him. His chuckle dribbles to a groan and his sliced thumb begins to throb. For a moment he'd forgotten the bed; he'd forgotten the chameleon; and he'd forgotten Alice. He'd like to say he'd forgotten Sam, too, but of course, he never forgets Sam.

Ten minutes later, if the man in the Land Rover had driven past, he wouldn't have known what to think. He'd have found Richard in the middle of the street staring straight up into that wide blue sky and asking himself the question it always came down to in the end.

SCENES FROM MY STUDY WINDOW

I CLICK ON Favorites and wait for the browser to pull up my bank's web page. When I hear Stefan on the steps of his condo, I look up, but for a second, I don't see him. Suddenly his skateboard hits the sidewalk with a sharp clank and he leaps on it from halfway up the stairs. Stefan plus his skateboard is a good thing. It means his step-dad Pollock didn't get drunk last night. Stefan minus his skateboard isn't so good.

My computer takes forever this morning to boot up, but what can I expect? It's seven years old, which in computer years is ancient.

Stefan glances at my study window but doesn't wave, and I wonder if he sees me through the glass. This time of year, I'm hard to spot. During the short winter days, it's still dark outside when I get up and my desk lamp is turned on, so I'm lit up like a Christmas tree. Now, at summer's end, it's already light outside and I don't need the lamp. Maneuvering through tiny lakes left from last night's rain, Stefan comes to a stop. He plants his right foot on the skateboard to set himself up. Since my checking account has yet to appear, I settle back to watch.

When Cam, my oldest, was twelve—Stefan's age—he broke his leg roller-skating. He and Stefan remind me of each other in looks. Stefan has his Swedish mother's blond hair. Cam inherited his straw-colored mop from me, but his lanky limbs are from his father. I don't often think of Cam now. The last I heard, he was someplace in Canada.

Stefan tries a fancy spin, hits a wet spot and the mystery of whether he sees me or not is solved. The first thing he does when his butt hits the ground is glance sheepishly at my window. I send him a three-fingered wave to assure him that despite the spill, he's still a fine skateboarder.

I type in my password. I'll check my bank balance first, then email, then work on my poetry that never sells. When my balance pops onto the screen, I'm comforted to see that no one has sabotaged my account during the night.

I love mornings, the stillness, the clarity of my thinking before the busyness of the day intrudes. I like winter mornings best when at dawn, daylight dilutes by subtle degrees the fading darkness. My study window faces east into the morning. Each spring, a cardinal appears in the Laurel oak outside. I don't know if it is the same bird year after year, but I welcome each as if it is.

Sally opens her patio door and steps outside. My building sits at the end of a U-shaped drive; she's on the right, the condo Stefan lives in is on the left. My study's double windows look out onto their buildings and the parking lot that separates them. A basket of begonias hangs from an oak limb; a Buddha squats nearby with a pot of Japanese impatiens residing in his belly. Fresh from last night's rain-bath, the plant's scarlet blossoms blaze like fire against the bronze metal.

Bending, Sally snaps a leash onto Jo-Jo, her puddle-brown and white Welsh corgi, who struts out behind her. I peer around the begonia to admire Sally's smooth unfurrowed brow. I know for a fact she's had it Botoxed, but I'm not telling. I say, good for her. Poverty keeps me wrinkled. If I win the lottery, the first thing I'll do is tack up every sagging part of me.

I jump when Samantha, my blue-eyed Siamese, springs into the rocker beside the desk. She perches, sizes up the situation. Finally, she leaps onto the desk and makes a nest between the phone and the picture of my late husband Austin.

We're alone now, Sam and I. Austin died six years ago. I've had five husbands in all. When I think of the insanity of that, I ask myself if perhaps my DNA is missing the gene that says, *Enough already!* I tease my daughter Christy, "So I had to kiss a lot of frogs." In reality, every morning now I bow in supplication to the powers that be. *Please keep me sane and single today.*

I bat at Sam, who nibbles on the pothos sitting next to the phone. I don't know if its poisonous or not, but that's beside the point. I don't want raggedy-eared plants. The poetry I write is about my pets—the dead ones, not the one who's alive. I write about them only when they've been gone for a while. Time and distance give me a perspective I wouldn't otherwise have. Except for Buckets, that is. Cam's miniature dachshund has been gone for years now, yet I haven't written a word about him.

Sally smiles when she strides past my window with Jo-Jo tripping along behind her. Speaking of husbands and insanity, Sally originally lived where she lives now. Then she married Budd and moved across the parking lot into his condo at the opposite end of the street. One night at midnight, he kicked her and Jo-Jo out. The story is Budd got fed up with dog hair. Apparently that night he found a stray one in his barley soup. I wonder, Who eats barley soup at midnight? So Sally wound up back in her condo, but the ruckus upset the entire complex. We're accustomed to quiet and quieter. Even Pollock keeps inside when he's drunk, except for the time he frog-marched Stefan to the dumpster with the trash, which hardly caused a stir since Pollock does that even when he's sober.

As for me, in my line-up of husbands, the first one, Cam's dad, was the worst. I lift my hands from the keyboard and extend them in front of me. The left index finger is only slightly larger now than the right. How to explain that? What do you say? *Oh, it accidentally ran into my husband's fist.*

Upstairs, I hear stirring, the baby fussing. It was quieter before Miss Greta moved. Although she'd traveled the world over with her husband who owned a huge construction firm, she had a surprising naivety that was disconcerting at times. I expected someone so well-traveled to be savvy about things she knew diddly-squat about. Don't get me wrong; she was smart. She was an expert at handiwork. Needlepoint, cross-stitch, she even knew how to tat and make beautiful lace. I have her lace doilies and cross-stitched coasters scattered all about. On the other hand, she practically developed apoplexy when she realized the guy who'd lived across the courtyard from her for years was gay. When he died, and she and I went through his belongings to find a next-of-kin, I had to explain the cookbook written for same sex couples we'd stumbled upon. I'd known all along our neighbor was gay. What I hadn't known was that homosexuals had their own cookbooks.

Sam makes a sneezing sound, I say "Gesundheit," and she nods a thank you. In my poems, I focus on the keen sixth sense of my pets; otherwise, poems about pets wind up as irksome blends of sappy sentimentality. When Sam is gone, I'll write volumes about her. She's remarkable, but stubborn, too. One of my husbands, the third one, was like that. Everything has to be their idea.

If I have any regrets about all of those husbands, it's the effect they had on Christy and Cam, especially Cam. No one needs that many stepfathers; no one needs that many husbands. There's no question, I could have been a better mother, but nothing I did made Cam do what he did to those children.

As the baby's cries grow louder upstairs, I prepare for what's coming. Last spring, at eighty-two, Miss Greta moved back to Yeehaw Junction. She went back pretty much the same person who'd left sixty years before, someone who thought you had to be married to get pregnant. She's the kind who made my mother shake her head and say, "Don't wake her up. Just let her sleep." But Miss Greta was a good neighbor. Every Friday while Austin was sick, she brought him a tomato sandwich—egg bread, slices of Big Boy tomato, salt, pepper and mayo—simple, just the way he liked them. Now, a young family—a chef, his wife and their new baby—lives upstairs. The father's name is Caesar. "Like the salad," he said when he introduced himself.

The baby starts bawling and I hear the dad yell, "All he does is cry!"

I take pride in the fact that, in time, my choice of husbands improved. I started out thinking *I'm going to fix him by damn or die trying* and finally learned that what I saw is pretty much what I got. Number two, Christy's father, was better than number one, but still no keeper. My husbands had reliability problems. With Austin, I hit the jackpot. He was as reliable as Elmer's glue. I'm glad. Otherwise, since he was the last, I might have wound up distasteful of men. And I like men, I always have. I enjoy the energy of the boy/girl thing. In fact, lust probably played a larger part in my number of marriages than I give it credit for. I'm a slow learner for sure, but finally it dawned on me that I can enjoy the company of men without having to marry them.

Austin's divorce from his first wife was difficult. "It's not the getting in that's the problem," he said. "It's the getting out." He informed me right off there wouldn't be any more divorces. "Maybe a killing or two," he said and laughed, "but no more divorces."

Our marriage was the best of the lot, but it was by no means perfect. Austin could be a challenge, but I say, who wants a man who's not? On our tenth anniversary, he gave me a pillow that said, *Some Days We Stay Together Merely For The Sake Of The Cat.* "Some days," I said, "that's enough."

I look up to see Stefan lean forward on the skateboard, give a push and off he goes. With his left leg pumping, he scoots across the pavement. He flies to the end of the lot, his stubborn blond hair—a crew cut growing out—sticks straight up. As he's about to crash into the curb, he suddenly flips the board. He pirouettes and lands balanced with one foot in front of the other. Then he sails toward me with a how-about-them-apples grin.

I knew Pollock before he started drinking again. He was a good man and thrilled to have a new wife and little boy and girl. Stefan was seven when Helene and Pollock married and Twila was two. She's a beautiful little girl except for a lazy eye that mars an otherwise perfect face. She hides her face in her mother's skirt as they climb the stairs. To his credit, Pollock didn't blame them when he began drinking again. He said he knew what he was getting into. He didn't, of course. Nobody does. It's absurd to think so.

Helene didn't speak a word of English when she and Pollock met. How they progressed as far as they did is beyond me. After they married, he wanted her to go to school, but she was from Sweden and loved to bake, so she wanted to work in a patisserie. "She's locked herself in the bedroom again," he said one day when I asked how things were going. A week later she'd unlocked the bedroom door, but now Pollock was in shock that not only did Stefan need braces, Helene's teeth needed straightening, too, plus both their mouths were full of cavities. All of that sugar in the pastries, the Lenten buns, the ones with cinnamon, the almond cookies, the strawberry cakes lavished in marzipan, I suppose. To make up for the lazy eye, the powers that be had given Twila perfect teeth. I don't know why Pollock was so surprised about the crooked teeth. He and Helene had dated for almost a year before they married. To hear him talk, you'd think neither Stefan nor she opened their mouths that whole time.

Finally Pollock cashed in his 401K and bought Helene a bakery. He said if she worked, she might as well work for herself. He was fifty-five when they married; she was thirty-four. When he turned fifty-seven, he was diagnosed with prostate cancer. How's that for unfair?

Outside, I see where last night's rain washed away the spider web that had stretched between the begonia and the oak. I thought I glimpsed an orange speck on the busy spider in the center of the web, but didn't lean close to make sure. The web looked so lovely spinning in the sunlight. I hated to tarnish that beauty with ghoulish black widow thoughts. Beside the web, chameleons had scurried up and down the tree trunk, their movements erratic, like the nervous stop and go of tiny robot cars. When I find one of the small creatures trapped inside the condo, I try to rescue it before Sam spots it. Austin used to laugh when I'd cup them in my hands and set them free outside. "Even a chameleon has a mother," I'd tell him. On the other hand, I douse snails with table salt and then feel like dancing a jig as they squirt their death juice and die, not caring in the least if they have a mother or not.

Yesterday I heard a commotion when I stopped for my lotto ticket at The Lucky Seven. Two young men, early twenties maybe, were scrapping it out on the pavement. Another standing nearby finally separated them. Muttering to himself, one of them turned and walked away. The other snatched a plastic bag of belongings from a junker car parked close by and threw it at the man. When it hit him in the back, he leaned down and picked it up. Then, with his shoulders slumped, he headed down the street.

I recognized the defeat in the drooped shoulders; I'd seen it before. The young man could have been Cam. For a second, I wanted to run after him, then stopped myself. *So, you catch him? What do you do then? Do you take him home with you?* The old trapped feeling closed around me, the despair in knowing that the day stretched out in front of you is a picture of the rest of your life. When he was here, Cam consumed my life; when he left, he dominated my thoughts. *Where's the freedom in that?* I thought as I pulled open the door to The Lucky Seven.

Cam excelled at looking pitiful. He came by it naturally. Before cell phones, it's what I did when I had car trouble on I-95. I'd raise the hood and stand by the roadside looking pitiful. It worked every time.

Cam's problems were no secret to Austin when he and I married. Cam was sixteen then and we were still in the house.

Later, when he was gone and Christy was away at college, we scaled down to this condo. Christy lives in New Smyrna now with Patrick and the two granddaughters. It's nice having them close.

Before Cam was fourteen, he'd set two fires in his bedroom, one in the family room and he'd lit Christy's Barbie Doll house on fire. At fifteen, he was expelled from the Ninth Grade Center for pulling a knife on another student in the lunch line. At sixteen, he'd stolen so much money from my purse, I kept it locked in our bedroom. At seventeen, he drowned Buckets in the swimming pool, broke Christy's left arm, and molested the two little Waldrop boys down the street.

Austin didn't try to take over; he stood back and let me do what I had to do. He watched me learn to look beyond the slumped shoulders to what came before and to weed through the excuses that fortified my denial. Christy's broken arm could have been an accident, but no matter how hard I tried to rationalize what happened down the street, I couldn't. Finally, by degrees, I came to face the truth about Cam. No matter how many times I bailed him out, that part of him that was broken was going to stay broken. It was a part I couldn't fix.

Back from their walk, Sally and Jo-Jo round the corner of the building and turn into her patio. With his short legs, it's hard for Jo-Jo to do much high-stepping, but he prances behind Sally like he's King of the Universe. Haughty Jo-Jo has made me question if Sally really got the raw deal from Budd that all of us in the complex were led to believe. As Austin used to say, there's his side and her side and what really happened. After Budd threw them out, I'd hear Sally whispering to Jo-Jo, "You are the sweetest doggie in the whole world, I don't care what anybody says."

The first time I hung up on Cam was the hardest. He called from an Oregon jail. "Mama, you've got to send money. They're going to hurt me bad if you don't."

I didn't ask who *they* were or how they planned to hurt him. "I'm sorry, Cam. I'm so sorry." Then I pressed the disconnect button. When I heard the dial tone, I wanted to reach through the phone and snatch back the words. *No! No! I didn't mean it. I promise, I'll send the money. Please don't hate me!*

I couldn't take the words back—a good thing in the end—I could only stare helplessly at the phone. As I stood, listening to the quiet, the weirdest sensation flooded through me. *Listen! Did you hear that? What was it? Oh, I didn't know a heart sounded like that when it broke.*

For a long time, I pictured the two little Waldrop boys curled in the fetal position, immobile forever. Then I saw them and they looked normal, whatever that is. At least they were functional. They were on the soccer team; they played tennis. I try to keep track of them—from afar, of course. I'm told that every stage in their development, they'll have to reexamine what happened to them. Then they'll either get past it or they won't. A child's saving grace is resiliency. One learns to hope it's enough.

When the weatherman forecasts a huge snowstorm for the far northeast, I sometimes think of Cam. I hope he's inside in a place that's warm. I hope he's not hungry. When the phone wakes me in the middle of the night, I check the caller I.D. Then I lie in the dark and listen to it ring and ring and ring.

Sometimes at night I hear Stefan practicing on his skateboard. The same *clank clanking* sound over and over tells me this is when he polishes his flips and twirls. With her lazy eye concealed in darkness, Twila sits at the top of the stairs and applauds her brother's fancy moves. Often I'll sit in the dark and watch him from my study window. By the light of the moon, his spins and twirls are graceful and true, a flawless moonlight ballet.

Now and then, after Stefan and Twila have gone inside, I linger at my window. I watch the condo lights flicker out, one by one. Some nights as the last one blinks off, Budd slides out of his back door with his pillow tucked under his arm. He skirts the parking lot, sticking in the shadows that rim the edge. When I hear his tap on my patio door, I stand for a moment as if weighing whether or not to let him in. Then I move through the darkened rooms. When I reach the patio, I unlock the door and he steps inside.

THE HURTING'S THE SAME

ONE TUESDAY WHEN I stayed after school taking my turn to dust erasers, our sixth-grade teacher Miss Sally looked up from her desk where she was grading papers. "You know, Amos," she said, tapping her thumbnail idly against the desktop as though she'd been in deep thought about a dilemma and had just stumbled on the solution. "Tomorrow is the best day of the week. It's called hump day, because when you get past Wednesday, it's downhill from there to Friday."

On the far side of the room, I clapped erasers together, watching the dust drift down like sifted flour. The fall days were fading into winter now, and the rays of sunlight pouring through the casement windows overhead were so sharp and pointed, they hurt my eyes when I tried to look at them head on. So I ducked my head out of their fierce glare and didn't answer back, but as far as I was concerned, Miss Sally was right. Not about it being the best day, just the hump part. Because Wednesdays are the days, while the sun is still slanted toward early morning, Daddy pulls his John Deere into the shed side of the barn and changes from his khaki work pants into his blue dress slacks and then heads in to Crown Hill with Mr. Ranew to do the bookkeeping at the stockyard. And Mama gets drunk while he's gone.

I'm naturally a chipper person in the morning. It's like I have a stopper that keeps the good feeling inside during the night, and when I come awake, I feel like doing a jig. But sometimes, either late every Tuesday or early Wednesday morning, the stopper comes unplugged and when I wake up, the good feelings has leaked out and what's left is a dread that sits like unleavened bread in my stomach. The closer the time comes for Mr. Ranew's red pickup to come back across the cattle gap at the end of the lane, the heavier the bread sits. I don't ever know what Daddy's liable to do when he comes home and finds Mama that way again. I don't think he knows what he's liable to do either. He gets awful mad sometimes. He never yells or throws stuff the way I've heard some people do, but his eyes turn a dull black like they're coated with something, and his bottom lip twitches. You can hardly see the twitch unless you know what you're looking for.

All of the Wednesdays are bad, even after Mama finally goes to bed and the quiet around the supper table becomes so heavy and burdensome, making us wish she was still up stumbling over chair legs and acting silly. But there was one Wednesday that was worse than all the others put together. Something happened that day that put a hurting in my chest like the time my puppy, Andy, stuck his head out just as Daddy brought the post-hole digger down. Andy made a grunting sound, and Daddy stepped quick between him and me. He stood still for a minute, looking down, then turned and sent me to the house on the run. I was four, maybe five, too little to understand what had happened, but old enough to know it was something bad.

Samuel was two at the time, Olivia—who we called Oreo for short—was in second grade, and I was twelve going on thirteen. On my way home from school that day, I sat by myself on the back seat of the bus. I blew on the window and then cleaned off a spot in the damp vapor to see outside better. When we rounded the bend past the Sutlive Place, I saw Mama waiting for us on the front porch. I punched the glass with my fist, sorry I hadn't left it dirty. Then I thought, *Who are you kidding, dummy? It's not like you didn't know.*

Mama had untied her apron strings and stood with her hands up, working with her hair. She caught the loose strands together and anchored them with a bobby pin in a knot at the back of her head. While I watched her fiddle with her hair, her face wavy through the streaked glass, I thought back to earlier that morning when Daddy had stood on the back porch in his slacks and undershirt, swishing water over his face from the washbasin. He said the same thing he says every Wednesday. "Mary Grace, get out my long-sleeved dress shirt. Mr. Ranew is due to pick me up directly." Daddy is proud of his good head for figures and spruces up for his bookkeeping job in Crown Hill.

He struck out for the front when Mr. Ranew tooted his horn. With the palm of his hand, he slicked back his hair to smooth over the teeth marks where he'd run a wet comb through it. His hair, too long and in need of a haircut, cupped each ear. At the truck, he propped his foot on the running board and looked back at Mama, who watched from behind the screen door. "You gonna behave yourself today, aren't you, girl?"

The question hung there, between them caught like the dust motes spinning in the sunlight, then it glanced off the kudzu vine choking the porch rail and bounced between them. *You gonna . . . You gonna . . .* When she finally nodded, I wondered if she meant it. If she did, she wouldn't be standing on the front porch when we got off the school bus. She'd be waving to us from the backyard where she'd be taking wash off the clothes line or potting fresh verbena cuttings in old coffee cans to root.

When I spied Mama now through the little patch I'd cleared in the windowpane, I knew this wasn't one of those days. I said to myself, *You lied again, Mama, what you said was a lie.* Oreo would say she'd told a fib or she'd told a story. But I'd gotten too old to fool with words that didn't say what they meant. Instead I spoke the truth, even though I knew the words would give me stomach cramps and make my insides churn. I clutched the window frame and held on tight, my knuckles white like the metal as the words spilled through my head. *When you do that Mama, do you do it to make*

147

him feel better or just to get him off your back? Or do you mean it, Mama? Are you lying to yourself, too?

When the school bus dropped me and Oreo off on the other side of the cattle gap, I straddled the ruts and stubbed my toes in the red clay, taking my time getting to the house.

"Amos, get Samuel and Oreo in the truck," Mama said as soon as we got in hearing distance.

I cut through a patch of gall berry bushes at the edge of the yard. The bushes whipped back against my dungarees, leaving dark stains down both pants legs. Any other time Mama would have cried, "And just who do you think is going to get that mess out of those pants, young man?" Now she just looked at me as I went inside and slung my books on the settee like I hadn't heard her tell me to fetch Samuel and Oreo.

"Come on, Amos," she said softly. "I'll buy you a Fig Newton."

When I got to the back room, Oreo had Samuel bouncing on the bed. Samuel squealed as he slid down into the corner where the slats were broken and the mattress lay at a slant on the floor. Me and Oreo had busted the slats last winter, jumping on the bed to touch the ceiling. If you looked, you could still see our handprints over the bed. Daddy had been in a rocker on the front porch when he heard the thump. "How many times have I told you young'uns about jumping on that bed?" he said. "Now you can sleep on it broke for a spell."

He meant it. Even now, we still woke up every morning, scrunched up in knots in the corner of the bed. Daddy was like that sometimes.

Oreo watched as Samuel twisted and turned, trying to slide away from me. I dived for him and caught him around the ankle.

"We going?" Oreo asked.

"What does it look like?"

She dug in her satchel, pitched out books and pencils with the erasers chewed off. When the bag was empty, she hung it over her shoulder.

"What you taking that thing for?"

"Cause I want to," she said. Oreo was usually chipper, but now her sparkle was gone. Her mouth had what Mama called "a stubborn set" to it as she flounced out the door with the bag bobbing on her shoulder, leaving me to put on Samuel's shoes and tie them for him.

Mama always said I was the man of the house when Daddy wasn't home. People said I even looked like him with his long legs and hair that was hard to do anything with. That made me the one to go outside and scoop up two Dominica hens, flapping and scratching, and put them in the back of the truck in a croaker sack. *Some man I am! Why don't I tell her NO! I ain't going and you ain't neither.*

Oreo sat in the middle with Samuel straddling her legs. Mama reached over and tickled him in the ribs. He giggled and squirmed off Oreo's lap down onto the floorboard of the truck. With his cheeks puffed out, he reminded me of an adder snake. I propped against the door on my side, keeping my eyes on the hills of peanuts in the fields along the roadside. The vines looked like they were reaching out toward each other, aimed for the valleys between the straggly rows. We'd be hoeing weeds from them come next week. Dog fennel, clover, the odd bunch of wire grass. I breathed in the hot dirt smell rising between my toes.

As Mama pulled in at Mr. Prather's store, two field hands stepped out over the sill, drinking from bottles of NuGrape turned up in their hands. They laughed, goosed each other.

"Sit here 'til they leave, Amos. Then go ask Mr. Prather what he'll give for two domineckers." Mama had hung her sweater across her shoulders and she reached up then to touch the scar at her neck. She got the scar a while ago when Daddy swerved the truck to miss two of Mr. Sutlive's sows rooting in the road. Mama was pitched against the dashboard hard and the rose pin she'd worn got broke. The pin lay on top of her bureau now, squashed flat as a Mason jar lid. The bruise from it turned out petal-shaped, greenish-blue, then yellow, with a tiny cut jagging down from it. Now only the scar was left.

Daddy had felt bad about it. You could tell. Only time he'd ever hurt her and it wasn't intentional then.

She'd said, "Ah, Edward, wasn't your fault. I should've held on better."

She never could wear the pin again. From then on, she hung her sweater loose around her shoulders like she had it now.

"Go along, Amos," she said when the field hands moved on. "Get Samuel and Oreo a penny sucker, too."

I wrestled the sack out of the tailgate and rested it on a clump of Bermuda grass, wilted and brown from the dry spell. The hens started up, already scared from the bouncing of the truck and now more upset from my jostling the sack when I heaved it over the side. When they settled down, I stumbled up the steps.

A whiff of smoking tobacco met me at the door. My eyes adjusted to the dim and I finally made out Mr. Prather behind the counter. He had a can of Prince Albert tilted, tapping loose tobacco into a thin strip of paper. He rolled it up tight like a lead pencil and slid it along the tip of his tongue to seal it. Then he rasped a kitchen match along the sole of his shoe and lit up. He stretched out the routine, taking an extra long time with it while I stood and shuffled my feet. Once he'd taken a long draw off his cigarette, he finally leaned across the counter.

"What you got there, Amos?" he asked.

"Mama wants to know what you'll give her for two domineckers. Big ones, past the pullet stage," I said and plopped the sack down on top of a keg of nails.

"Well, let's take a look." He parted the open end of the sack and peeped in.

You know what they look like, ya old chicken thief. I stepped wide by mistake and kicked at a rope coiled beside the counter, tangling it with my toe. Mr. Prather didn't say anything. He grinned and took short, quick puffs off his cigarette.

On my way out, I stuck the penny suckers in my pocket, orange for Oreo, purple for Samuel, because he likes grape better. Mama had the motor running, afraid if she turned it off, it wouldn't crank up again. I chewed on a Fig Newton as I climbed in and slammed the door.

"Careful, Amos. Watch Samuel's fingers. Don't shut them in the door," she said, shifting into gear.

When we got to the liquor store, she glanced at it out of the corner of her eye as she drove on past. She always drove by one time slow to make sure nobody she knew was there. A little ways up, she wheeled into a dirt road and turned around, careful to stay out of the soft sand where she'd bogged down once.

"You young'uns stay here," she said, parking in back of the store under a pair of tall slash pines. She looked down at Samuel. He was half-asleep, his head lolling over Oreo's arm. Sweat ringed his top lip and a rim of dirt was caught in his neck creases.. Mama closed the door gently when she got out so as not to wake him.

We waited in the truck, Samuel sleeping, me and Oreo not saying a word. I hunched low, stared at the tar cup on one of the pines, resin dribbling down like dark glue. I prayed steady now, hoping nobody would see me. *Lord, please don't let anybody from school come by. I promise I'll be good from now on.* I wanted to say, *Don't let Jimmy Futch see me.* He lived about a mile down the road from the liquor store. When we sided up for baseball, he'd picked me to play first base the last two days in a row. It didn't seem right, my naming Jimmy in my prayers, so I used anybody, hoping the Lord would know who I meant.

"What you thinking?" Oreo asked. She shifted, propped Samuel's head up better on her arm.

"Nothing," I said, swiping at a knot of gnats that circled in front of my face. They swirled away, then sailed back.

"I wish Mama would hurry, is what I'm thinking. It's hot sitting still."

Mama stepped out of the door then, a brown paper sack tucked under her sweater. She looked straight ahead, walked fast.

Her feet made *swish, swishing* sounds on the pine needles scattered on the ground.

My eyes were even with the window when Mama spun the wheels in the loose gravel at the edge of the hardtop. She kept her eyes on the road until we passed Jimmy's house, then she looked over at me. I straightened up, stared out the window on my side like I was counting fence posts. I wasn't though. I already knew there were seventy-three from the liquor store to our house, that is, if you added the big one not holding up anything at the end of the lane.

As we neared home, I prayed faster. *Lord, let the bottle slip and break on the steps. It'll soak in around the roots of that bushy vine railing the porch. I'll pick up the pieces of glass and nobody will ever know the difference.*

I stopped praying a few hours later as I sniffed the empty glass on the kitchen counter and smelled the whiskey odor inside.

When Samuel came in for Mama to tickle him, she called, "Watch him, Oreo. Don't let him go toward the road. Ya'll play in the back yard."

Oreo did as she asked while I did chores, scattering chicken feed with the grain bag straddled to my shoulder. When I plucked two setting hens off their nests and felt for eggs, they cackled like a house a fire. Then I brought in a load of stove wood. I kept one eye on the dirt road that led up to the house while words swarmed like a beehive inside my head. *Please be late tonight, Daddy. One mistake is all it'll take. Then you'll have to go back over the books to make them come out right. She'll go to bed if you give her half a chance.*

Mama added water to the liquor in the glass, threw her head back, and swallowed quick. She made a face and put down the glass. Samuel came in to the kitchen crying, trying again for her attention. "Oh, baby," she said. She sat and pulled him up in her lap. "What's the matter with my baby?"

"I couldn't help it," Oreo said. She came up behind him crying, too. "He crawled under the house after one of Daffodil's kittens and got in an ant bed."

"Hush, Oreo." Mama brushed the dirt from Samuel's legs, then dabbed at the welts with Calamine Lotion, letting the pink drip down. She wiped between his toes, then wiggled them back and to. "This little piggy . . .this little . . . Please, Samuel, say it with me."

Samuel looked up at her, then slid off her lap, still whining. She stared at where he'd been in her lap, trying to focus. When she stood, light from the window suddenly split her face in half. One side of it was dim, with dark shadows rimming her cheek, while the other glowed with a sheen that gave her skin a polished look. When she caught the edge of the table to steady herself, I gripped the table, too. It was all I could do to keep from reaching up and touching her skin. I yearned to run my finger down the bridge of her nose, smooth my palm against each cheek, find which of them was real. My fingertips burned, then filled with a sudden numbness when she said, "See to him, Amos. I'm going to lie down."

She turned then, lurched against the dish cabinet, rattling the plates and saucers. When she stopped in the doorway and looked back at us, the light glanced away, leaving her face cloaked in shadow.

Outside in the dark, I heard through my bedroom window a bullfrog croak down by the creek—a sure sign of rain. Samuel made bubbly sounds in his sleep. I lay beside him and stared up at the ceiling, wondering what Daddy would do when he got home. Would he take Mama to Grandma Eleanor's? He'd done that once, rousting us out of bed in the middle of the night. A hard rain had just stopped and the red clay road had been slick. We'd slipped and slid, bracing our feet against the floorboard of the truck. He'd driven so fast he hardly made the curves in time to keep the truck from pitching over in the ditches.

Grandma Eleanor came to the door in her gown, her nighttime braid swaying down her back. When she saw who it was, she stepped out, holding the lantern over her head.

"What can I do, Miss Eleanor?" Daddy cried, beating his fist against the nose of the truck.

Grandma Eleanor came around to where Mama sat in the passenger seat, Samuel leaning close against her. She looked at Mama, the lantern light doing a jittery dance on the side of her face. Then she coiled a strand of hair behind Mama's ear, soft-like, and said, "Take her home, Edward. She'll be all right in the morning. It's in the blood. She was born with it . . . like her pa."

Meanwhile Mama made cooing sounds against Samuel's ear, like mourning doves when they're nesting.

"Edward, it's these Wednesdays. . ." Grandma Eleanor said.

"I've got to work at the stockyard. You know we need the money," Daddy said like he was mad at her for something.

"I know," Grandma Eleanor said, trying to quiet him. "I know."

I finally heard Mr. Ranew's truck cross the cattle gap, a quick rumble of thunder that sounded way off. I turned over, pulled my knees close to my chin. Mama had switched on the light in the front room. I heard her stirring around, then the front door slam.

"My God, Mary Grace! Not again! I can't go off one day . . ."

Mama giggled. I covered my head with my pillow, jamming it down over my ears like a stopper.

"Lie down and go to sleep. You're not making a bit of sense. I'm tired, for God's sake . . ."

It sounded like Mama wanted to tell him something and he wouldn't listen.

"You going? Where?" he said with a short laugh. "Your own ma don't want you drunk. You're not going in there where those young'uns are, either."

I heard feet moving around fast, then slapping sounds. Mama cried out sharp, then made a low whining sound, the kind Daffodil's kittens make when they're hungry. That's when I got the hurting in my chest, the same hurting I got when Andy was killed by the posthole digger. It wouldn't go away, I don't care how many long deep breaths I took. I sat up straight in bed and my head bumped Oreo's in the dark.

"He hit her!" she whispered.

"Shh."

"Let's run away." Oreo was crying hard. "Come on," she said. I heard her pull her book satchel out from under the bed.

"We can't. What about her?"

"I'm scared, Amos. Can I get in bed with you and Samuel?"

I turned back the covers and she slid in next to me. We lay in the dark listening while streaks of filmy light from traffic on the hard road played like ghost fingers across the ceiling.

Mama fried bacon with her hand up against her face over the blue mark. While Samuel clacked a case knife on the arm of his high chair, wanting another biscuit, Daddy ate in a hurry, his head bent over his plate of grits. When he finished, he scraped his chair back from the table and pushed through the screened door, holding it behind him so it wouldn't slam. He walked over to the clothes line and propped against the post. Mama had hung some wash out early and he stood, watching it crack and flap in the morning breeze. He glanced back at the kitchen window once, then headed for the tractor-shed side of the barn.

I drank my milk but left the bacon crumbled in a crusty pile on my plate. Mama sat in the chair across the table from me while I ate. From the corner of my eye, I could see she had yet to put her hair up, and it swung loose around her shoulders.

"Amos," she said. She was quiet for a minute, then she said, "Sometimes people are forced to do things they'd just as soon not."

You lied, I wanted to yell, *you lied again*, but all I did was keep my eyes on my plate.

"Look at me, son."

I looked up. Some hairs had caught in her blouse button. She worked at them with her fingers. A shadow shaped like a half-moon was on the side of her face. Another one that looked like a pine burr rested on the back of her hand.

"You'll remember that, won't you?"

I kept my eyes on the hand twisting the hairs back and to and never said a word.

At lunch, I leaned my back against the trunk of a sweet gum tree at the side of the playground. I picked up a leaf that had drifted down and studied it. Somebody stirred in the leaves. I looked up to see Jimmy settle down and make a nest beside me.

"You missed recess," he said.

"Had homework."

"Gerald played first. Dropped two."

"Yeah?"

Three little girls from second grade sailed down the slide close to us.

Their laughing sounded loud now that me and Jimmy weren't saying anything. I pulled the leaf through my fingers, felt the rough edges catch on the sweat in my hand.

"Jimmy," I said, kind of low.

"Huh?"

"Did . . . did your daddy ever hit your mama?"

Jimmy looked up from digging in his lunch pail and shook his head. I thought he might ask why I wanted to know, so I didn't look up until I heard him rustling in his lunch pail again.

I sat thinking until the bell rang. It being midday, Daddy probably had the peanuts plowed by now and you had to look real hard anymore to even see the scar the rose pin had made on Mama's chest. She was always telling me my dungarees looked like they were about to wind up down at my knees, so before I went inside, I hiked them up good around my waist.

Miss Sally showed us how to do reading problems on the blackboard after lunch. When she told us to, I turned to the word problem on page thirty-nine, just like everybody else.

THE INTRUDER

HALLIE HEARS THE first knock as she stands in the bathroom in her bra and panties brushing her teeth. It's a tentative tap, barely audible over the water gushing into the sink. When she turns off the faucet and runs her tongue over her minty teeth, the second knock comes, louder and more distinct.

"Tom, someone is at the door. You'll get it?"

"Not this late. Someone wants to see me, they'll get here before eleven at night," Tom says from the bedroom. The stubborn note in his voice is one Hallie knows not to argue with. He sounds tired. He owns the only independent hardware store in town and at sixty-five and overweight, working all day on his feet isn't easy. He'd loved to have had a son to turn the business over to, but a case of mumps in his late teens took care of that. He'd insisted that she help out at the store once she'd retired as librarian at Tyson High. Hallie relinquished her idea of a quiet life of reading after retirement and stood these days behind the counter ringing up toilet plungers and toggle bolts. Her life was easier when she did as Tom asked.

"Suit yourself," she says and drops her toothbrush back into the holder. When she hears the front door knob turn, however, she looks up sharply at Tom. He has his head cocked to one side, listening, too.

"Who do you think it could be?" she asks, her voice lower now. The master bedroom sits at the back of the condo, but the place is small and the front door isn't that far away.

"I don't like the sound of that." Tom had been sitting on his side of the bed taking off his shoes and socks. Now he edges closer to the bedside table, and Hallie stiffens. A gun lover and staunch believer in the right to defend—not that he'd ever had to, but still—he has guns stationed all over the house just in case. His father's double barrel shot gun, the single shot rifle his grandfather left him, the tiny pearl inlaid hand gun he keeps in the bedside table drawer. Years ago, in a foolish accident they don't discuss, he shot himself through the right calf practicing his quick draw. It left him with a slight limp. The tiny handgun was supposed to be Hallie's, but she'd have nothing to do with it—the only time she'd had the courage to tell Tom no. Even now, the idea of pointing a gun at someone puts a knot in her stomach. She's tried ignoring the guns, tried to remember her mother's sage advice about how wisdom is knowing what to overlook. When they first met, she felt a hint of something she couldn't identify in Tom, something that simmered beneath the surface, threatening always to boil over. It excited her then, from the moment Tom, the type of man who wouldn't ordinarily look twice at her, marched arrogantly across the dance floor and stopped in front of her rather than Connie Maxwell, who stood beside her, as thin as a letter opener with jutting breasts.

"My name is Grady Donaldson and I've always wanted to live on the corner of Grady and Donaldson Street," Tom had said. Of course, his name wasn't Grady Donaldson—it was Tom, she was to learn later—but who could resist a pick up line like that? Not Hallie, the new librarian, a shy blonde who'd just moved into a first floor apartment at 22 E. Grady Street, a building located on the corner of Grady and Donaldson.

"May I have this dance?"

"With me?" Hallie asked.

"You!" he replied and aimed an index finger at the imaginary bull's eye stationed over her heart.

With her toes pinched together in pointed sling-backs, she fell in love with him then, marveling at his perfect teeth and the thick brows that hung shelf-like over his bottle-green eyes. To this day, she's never stopped being grateful to him for choosing her over Connie and her stellar breasts.

A thunder of sound breaks the quiet, a banging so loud the condo trembles She hears from the living room what sounds like a wine decanter shatter. Tom whips the tiny handgun from the drawer. He walks barefoot to the door of the bedroom.

"Who's there?" he yells.

The racket stops. A cold chill runs through Hallie when she remembers that Mr. Chambers in the upstairs condo is still out of town. He's not due back until the day after tomorrow. She shrugs into her robe and pulls it closely around her shoulders.

"Who is it?" Tom yells again, his voice an angry roar and his eyes like huge black holes in his face. When his eyes turn black, the dark centers expanding until they obliterate the bottle green, Hallie never knows what he'll do. What she does know is that he's capable of anything.

Fifteen years ago, when his feet became tangled as he whirled to block her from leaving the kitchen—*Don't you dare walk away from me when I'm talking to you*—he'd stumbled and fallen, the bone in his arm snapping like a birch twig when he hit the floor. She hadn't believed him when he groaned through gritted teeth, "If my arm is broken, I'm telling them you did it." She should have believed him.

He embellished the accident, turning it into a tale of domestic violence in which the police were called and she'd wound up threatened with incarceration. And of course, what she told the detective about the incident probably hadn't helped her case. She hadn't pushed Tom, but she'd been so mad she'd felt like it.

Suddenly the noise at the front door begins again, but different now. Rather than the pounding, Hallie hears what sounds like a

159

heavy object slam against the door. Tom yells over his shoulder, "Call 911!"

Hallie lifts the phone just as the front door splinters. She is so startled, she fumbles and drops the phone to the floor. Scrambling beside the bed on her hands and knees, she grabs it. Her fingers are numb. She has trouble dialing the number. Ring! Ring! Ring! *Please answer, please answer,* she prays. Behind her, she hears the door rip from its hinges.

"I have a gun! You come inside, I'll blow your head off!" Tom yells.

When the operator finally comes on the line, Hallie's thoughts are jumbled. Where are we? What's our address? At last she stammers, "Someone is breaking down our front door. Yes! Yes! Stonehenge Condo Complex. Number 802. Hurry! Hurry! Please!"

Tom is in the hallway now. "I'm telling you. I have a gun. You come through that door, I'll kill you!"

A wave of nausea hits Hallie and she swallows quickly. Tom's voice is calm and full of steel. He's not afraid. He's furious.

With a savage roar, the intruder slams through the door. He is young, twenty-three or twenty-four, and huge, so big that his body fills the narrow hallway as he lumbers toward them. The grimace on his face is one of fixed determination. Is the man insane?

The first bullet hits him in the chest, the second in the neck below his chin. Blood spurts from the tiny hole and sprays the wall above the thermostat and the closet door. He keeps coming, bulldozing his way down the hall. Tom shoots again. The man stops and stares down wide-eyed at the blood bubbling from the hole in his stomach. He clutches his belly and crumples to the floor, crashing forward like a huge oak. His head lands with a thud inches away from Tom's feet.

Methodically, Tom points the gun at the back of the man's head and pulls the trigger. One. Two. Three. Finally, when the chamber clicks empty, he looks up at Hallie, his face twisted in rage.

She stares at him, her hand clasped over her mouth to hold back a scream. The odd smell of cordite crowds the air around her. Finally she whispers, "Did you have to shoot so many times? Did you have to kill him?

"No, actually I could have winged him in the left arm so he could've raped you using only his right," Tom says with a sneer. Then, as Hallie watches in disbelief, he lifts the pistol and blows on the end of it like a gunslinger in a Western movie.

Later, when the body has been taken away, the mess of blood cleaned from the walls and carpet, and everything is back to normal, the scene keeps playing itself over in Hallie's mind. The huge intruder crashing down the hall, Tom shooting the man in the back of the head again and again, and Hallie asking the questions she didn't ask before. *Who is this man? Do you know him?*

When she and Tom and the young man he'd shot can no longer live together, she leaves.

Every now and again, on a night before the sleeping pills kick in and Hallie forgets to direct her thoughts into safe places, she's suddenly struck by the minty taste of toothpaste on her tongue. She's back watching Tom lift the gun to his lips and blow on the barrel. She sees the simmering inside of him finally erupt and is astounded once again at how he relishes every second of the kill.

I'M HERE, MR. SULLIVAN

"YOU'LL LET ME know if the pills don't help," the nurse says as she dims the light over his bed.

Nodding that he's heard, Sullivan watches as she steps through the door and closes it behind her. He likes this nurse. She does the things that need to be done and leaves. She doesn't fuss over him as the others do, and as his wife does. *My, how much better you look. Here, let me fluff that pillow.* He knows what they're doing and wishes they wouldn't. Stillness and silence is what he yearns for now.

The pain is bad, coming in waves that leave him breathless. With his body covered in sweat, he waits for relief. As he waits, his thoughts drift to the children in the ward next door. A moment before, several of them were crying. When his pain is at its worse, his senses are keen, his mind precision clear. The children's wailing tunnels down into the core of him, below his waist, to the place in his back where the throbbing lives. Finally the children grow quiet.

He's learned to be grateful for small things: the perky light from the hallway before a purposeful someone closes the door; the striated petals on the leaves of the camphor tree outside his window; a smoothed toenail that doesn't catch in the sheets.

A priest dropped by yesterday. This is a Catholic hospital, St. Joseph's, so it wasn't the cleric's first visit. The difference is that, yesterday, he was summoned. Not by me, Sullivan thinks. He has no problem with what Father O'Brien is selling. It's simply an avenue he's never pursued—and won't now. It would be unfair somehow, unthinkable without having paid one's dues beforehand. He thinks he knows the feelings the priest is talking about—a buoyant freeing sensation, a feeling he's experienced before when he snagged a wide-mouthed bass or took his early morning walks. Someone once called walking a process of falling forward, but it's more than that. He thinks of it as his briskly efficient body in its singing mode. He wiggles his toes at the thought. He'll miss that, and before the walks each morning, the toasted English muffin with cream cheese, the whipped kind spread thinly to save his arteries, and the coffee that smells so much better than it tastes. He laced it with flavored creamer, Irish Cream, and two packets of artificial sweetener. When his wife reprimanded him, he joked with a cocked eyebrow, *So the mice and I get cancer.*

The doctors told him at first the pain was sciatica. Now here he is.

He glances toward the bedside table at his lighted clock that flips away the seconds. Two a.m. The bedclothes feel heavy on his legs, cramping his toes. He shifts restlessly and pushes down until his feet touch the end of the bed. He knows how long it takes for the pills to work. They begin subtly, then gather until their soft tentacles lull him into a brief sleep. He's never completely separated from the pain, but the pills keep it tolerable.

Turning his head, he finds a new spot on the pillow and listens to the building settle down for the night. He hears the faint rattle of a stretcher as it *clack clacks* down the hall. Someone giggles. The sound stops shortly as though whoever giggled suddenly remembered that this is a hospital, that it's the middle of the night.

In the eerie quiet, he listens and waits. Waiting is the hard part. The pain drains his energy and leaves him exhausted with little strength to keep his thoughts at bay. He believes the pain heightens his senses; the nurses say it's the effect of the chemo.

Either way, his thoughts seem to take on a smell, a rank odor that leaves a sour metallic taste on his tongue.

He is forty-five years old and he is about to die. Those who are forty-five and who are not about to die might think, *It could be worse. At least you've lived some. Think how you'd feel if you were twenty or twelve.*

At one time he'd have agreed. But he's dying. Can he help if he looks at death differently now? It's only one of the many things he looks at differently now.

He's surprised at the odd comfort he's found in understanding that the cancer has won. Not that he wants to die, of course. But to finally abandon his delusion that he might win took the fight right out of him. At first, he was filled with rage at the unfairness that he wouldn't be here for his forty-sixth birthday, his forty-seventh. What had he ever done to anyone to deserve this? Next came the sitting on the fence, of not knowing if he'd live or die. One day he'd think, *I know I'm going to die*, but on the next day, he'd reconsider, *well, maybe not*. Then reality set in. What remarkable peace came from simply climbing down off the fence and relinquishing hope. And with the delusion went the anger. What he resents now is having to die alone. His wife and son won't admit that the cancer has won.

The drowsy feeling takes over and his lids sag. His eyes feel grainy, like sand is caught behind the lids. If he rubs them, the gritty feeling will disappear, but before he can lift his hand, he drifts. A boggy softness closes around him. As he's about to slip away, he feels a light touch on his arm. For a second he holds very still. Is he mistaken? Then someone whispers, "Mr. Sullivan, are you awake? Wake up."

He opens his eyes and tries to focus.

"I'm here, Mr. Sullivan." The words are tense and urgent.

Shaking his head, the cloud cloaking his vision separates and he sees a little girl standing beside the bed. A little girl! He shakes his head again and stares. Yes, he thinks he sees a little girl beside the bed, cradling a Kleenex box in her arms. Is he hallucinating? He can't be sure.

A buzzer sounds outside in the corridor. He hears quick footsteps and low excited voices. So he's not hallucinating. He reaches for the call light. When he does, the little girl leans close and places a finger to her lips. "Sh—h-h," she whispers.

The noise fades outside.

"Wh-o-o are you?" he asks, blinking.

Before she answers, the little girl places the box carefully on the bed beside him. He peers inside. On a bed of folded tissues rests a ragged doll with red hair. The doll's yarn hair is raveled at the end of each braid and one of its button eyes hangs loose. Working meticulously, the little girl settles the Kleenex box between two wrinkles in the blanket and tucks a thin sheet snugly around the doll's shoulders. Then she looks up. "My name is Annie."

He raises himself on one elbow and looks at her more closely. He's amazed at how tiny she is; her head barely tops the rumpled blanket. Her huge brown eyes smudged in sooty circles consume a pale, narrow face. A hospital gown with jumping brown bears peeks from beneath a furry robe. When she sweeps her blond hair back from her face, he sees that the skin on her hand is bruised and her nails are ragged and bitten. Although she is tiny and frail, her shoulders are straight. Tapping her finger against the Kleenex box, she plays a little tune while she waits for him to finish studying her.

"Do I know you, Annie?"

"I don't think so." She props her elbow on the bed. She cups her chin in her palm and sits studying his face. Finally she says, "I never saw anybody like you before, somebody who's going to die. Jennifer in the next bed to me died, but I didn't know she was going to, so it doesn't count."

He gazes down at her, startled.

"You are going to die, aren't you, Mr. Sullivan?" she asks, her eyes as deep as pond water.

He lowers his head until it rests on the pillow and looks up at the ceiling. "Yes, I suppose I am."

"That's what my daddy said to my mommy today when we walked by your room. The lady who comes to see you was outside in the hall. She was crying hard." Annie paused, then went on. "My mama cried once, too. They thought I was asleep. My daddy cried when he got off work. My brother hasn't cried yet. He's fourteen."

"Your brother hasn't cried?"

"No."

"Oh."

"He's going to have a birthday party." Now she looked up at the ceiling, too. "I probably won't be going."

"Why?"

"It's not 'til September."

His heart drums in his chest and at the back of his neck and in his ears—the way it does when the pain is at its worse. Yet surprisingly, his really hard severe pain remains at bay. When it stays away and shows itself only fleetingly, he can think fairly clearly. Taking a slow, deep breath, he says, "I don't think I'll be going to my son's birthday party either. He'll be twenty-four."

Annie's eyes fly open wider. "Gosh, he's old."

"Yeah, he's real old. Lots older than you. How old are you?"

"Six, going on seven. He's nice now."

"Who?" He breathes more easily now, but his palms are sweaty. He presses them flat against the sheet.

"My brother."

"Oh."

Annie wiggles the Kleenex box to one side and starts to pull herself up onto the bed. When she sees him wince, she stops. "Does it hurt when I lean?"

"Not when you lean."

She smoothes her doll's fuzzy braids. "I can eat candy before dinner. Even when I don't eat my carrots. Are they nice to you, too?"

"Yeah."

Annie glances at the doll nestled in the box then stares down the length of the bed at his legs outlined beneath the sheet. "You sure are long. Will they bend your knees to get you in your box?" Without waiting for a reply, she says, "I had to bend Raggedy Ann's legs to get her in her box. She fits fine now. Will they get a extra long one for you?"

He looks down at the slight bend in the doll's knees, then shifting, he follows Annie's gaze. I am real long, he thinks, chuckling to himself.

"I don't know. Guess I need to check on that."

"I'll bet they get a real long one. They'll just need a little one for me. I'm little."

Peering down at her, he says, "You sure are."

"Forty-eight pounds. They weighed me this morning."

Annie toys with the covers, running her fingers over the rough edge of the sheet. "You think it's cold in the box?"

Before he can answer, she goes on. "I'll bet it's real dark."

He watches her face in the faint light. "Yeah, probably."

When she doesn't answer, he brings his hand from beneath the sheet and moving it slowly across the bed, he places it beside her hand. He looks at the two hands, palms up, side by side. Lying this way, the bruises are hidden; the hands could belong to anyone. Gently, he touches her arm.

"Are you scared?" he asks.

For a moment, Annie is quiet. Then, in a tiny voice, she says, "A little. It's . . ."

Pausing, he takes a deep breath. "Know something? I was scared, too."

"Oh, yeah?"

"Maybe everybody's scared."

She leans closer. "Maybe, you think?"

"Yeah."

"Maybe I won't be scared anymore either, you think?"

"I hope not, Annie."

Rubbing her hand back and forth across her forehead, she says, "My head hurts sometimes. Does yours?"

"Sometimes. I hurt more back here," he replies, shifting and pointing to his back. "The nurse gave me some pills. They help."

"Once they used a needle to put some medicine here," she says, lifting her bruised hand. "The medicine came down a tube from high up in a bottle."

He nods. "I had that, too."

"Miss Betty, she's the nurse who puts the needles in, says I don't have very good veins."

She pushes up the sleeve of her robe. Her frail arm is thin with fading bruises from the elbow to her wrist. He looks quickly away.

"Do you?" she asks.

"Do I what?"

"Have good veins?"

"I guess so." He moves his gown aside and examines his forearm. One small scab nestles in a wrinkle of skin at his wrist.

"You're real skinny."

"I used to be fat before. . ."

"Oh."

Annie glances around the room. "If I get scared again, it'll probably be at night. I get real scared at night when it's dark," she whispers.

"I know." He follows her gaze to the dark corners of the room. Suddenly he thinks of holding his son Jackie when he was six while the doctor sutured the cheek laceration. Sullivan remembers the pieces of mulch still caught in the creases of the boy's neck. How quickly his panic at the blood had disappeared when he rested his hand against Jackie's hair, ruffled as goose down on his head.

Sullivan turns his hand and cups it over Annie's. "Annie, it's soft in the box."

"You think so?" she asks earnestly, her fingers curling into his palm.

"Absolutely. I'm positive."

"Like this?" She touches the sleeve of her robe.

"Like that."

For a long time, Annie stands fingering the soft edge of her robe. Then she slips her hand free from his cupped palm and picks up the Kleenex box. He feels the beat in his chest again, but slow and steady now as he watches her tuck the edge of the doll's skirt inside. She props the box under her arm and tiptoes to the door. At the doorway she turns. "You're sure, Mr. Sullivan?"

"I'm sure."

She settles the box against her hip and pulls open the door. Leaving the door slightly ajar, she slides out of sight. A slice of light fans across his knees. Shifting his legs, he watches the light bend and turn. He stretches his long arm toward the foot of the bed to catch the dizzy play of light in his outstretched hand.

A WHITE LINEN SUIT

THE MAN CALLS early in the morning. "Meet me on the corner of Brighton and Long at twelve," he says. He spits out the words, short and clipped, with a rusty sound as though his voice hasn't been used yet today. There is no small talk, no how-dee-do. Only *Meet me on the corner of Brighton and Long at twelve.* Click!

So at twelve sharp, I'm waiting on the corner.

He's a big man. I mean gargantuan. Thick neck, hams for arms. I'm not a big man. I'm a little man with a hint of five o'clock shadow if I don't shave—maybe. The guy sits in a white Cadillac convertible in a white suit with a white Panama hat shading his eyes. Except for his size and the look on his face, he reminds me of a photograph I saw once of Truman Capote. He was dressed in pure white, too. Capote sat in a convertible similar to this one. His arm was slung across the windowsill in the same careless way. He had that smirk on his face, the one with the sly smile that said *I know some dirt about somebody that you don't.*

The man in front of me isn't smiling. I get a funny feeling in my stomach and ask myself if what I'm doing is smart. Maybe I should forget it. Then I think, no, too much hangs on this meeting for me to walk away now.

I'm a writer and I'd like to spend time with writers. But I have a problem. I don't know any writers. I mean, I don't know any in real life. I feel like I do, but I don't, not in the honest-to-God flesh. Then there's the other problem. I don't have anything to write about. Sure, I have lots of things I *could* write about, but to nail down one idea and run with it, that's tough. So I spend most of my time sitting and staring. Or I do squirrelly stuff like rub my hand over and over the bald spot on my head, hoping to stimulate something up there—maybe.

One morning I found myself hunched in front of the computer screen, clueless again. If I snatched one concrete thought from the whirlwind of ideas spinning through my head, I'd make progress. I tried to grab one and hold it up for some prolonged examination, but no luck. I couldn't dig out a premise that worked. I couldn't execute. Instead I sat and stared. Crazy!

Suddenly I said to myself, I know what I need. I need a writer's group. So next morning, I put an ad in the paper that read, *Needed! Writers to talk writing!* Simple. Just like that. And this guy calls up. Now here I am, face to face with a man as big as Mount Rushmore dressed in white linen.

He doesn't get out of the car or say hello. He leans his great ham hock of a shoulder against the door and says, "I got this book I'm writing. Need somebody to look at it. You look at it."

"I'm not an editor. I only brought this along in case I got an idea while I was out," I say, pointing to my laptop. "I don't edit. I'm just looking to start a writer's group."

"I'll bring it for you to look at," he says as though I haven't opened my mouth. "Be here tomorrow. Same time." He jerks the car in gear and peels away from the curb.

So the next day I meet this guy at the same time. Am I stupid or what? You tell me.

At twelve he drives up. The top is down on the convertible again. It's stifling, over a hundred, the heat melting into thick waves of hot vapor. He hands two cardboard boxes out the window. They look heavy and are tied with strings ending in bows that stick up like insect antennae.

"What you need is an editor," I tell him again.

Deliberately he eases the boxes down to rest against the window. Then he says in his gravelly voice, "It's taken me seventeen years to write this book. Do you know how long seventeen years is?"

I nod. I know, really I do.

"I've had a hundred and sixty-one rejections."

"Drive around the corner," I say. "Just drive around the corner and park. I'll meet you. We'll talk."

When he doesn't move, I say, "I really think you need an editor. I'm not an editor. I can't . . ." My words trail off.

He doesn't bat an eye. "I have a gun. If you don't look at my book, I'll kill you." The words are soaked in nonchalance, but I do not doubt that he means them.

I don't move.

He leans out the window and tosses the boxes into the street. *Thud!* They hit the concrete hard. The sides of the boxes flip open. Loose pages scatter like paving stones.

I turn and begin to walk away.

"Hey, egghead, you think I'm kidding? I'll shoot."

I do not think he is kidding. What am I doing? I can't believe what I'm doing. I am not a brave man. Still I keep walking.

Behind me I hear shots. One, two. *Crack! Crack!* He wings the concrete building on my left. People scream. I hear them scramble for cover.

I keep walking. Three. The bullet whistles past my left ear. Sweat pops out on my forehead. I wonder what kind of gun he's using, how many shots it holds.

Slowly, slowly I walk. Don't look back. And for God's sake, don't run! And I don't. I don't run.

I see an opening on my right. I turn into it. I move at a slow easy pace. My arms swing loosely at my sides. My armpits are drenched. Sometimes you just know what to do. You don't know how you know, you just do. Not all of the time, but sometimes.

The opening I've turned into is a long narrow alley. Miles of brick wall tower upward. I spot a cube of sky overhead. At the end of the alley, a tiny speck of light appears. I walk toward the speck. The brick walls lean in on either side of me. I hear sirens. The whining sound fades in and out. A hollow echo bounces off the bricks and weaves itself around me.

At the end of the alley, a light shines bright as a flashlight beam. It's a window. Steaks of fine sunlight struggle through the dusty panes. That's odd, an alley that ends in a brick wall with a window.

It's scorching in the alley. I fan out my shirt behind me to catch a breeze. I think of the man. He'd flipped the boxes out of the car window like flicking ashes off the tip of a cigar.

Seventeen years. Man, that's something. What was he thinking all those years? Then no, no, no, one hundred and sixty-one times. Man!

I pick up speed now. My arms swing out, wide and looping. I grab at gulps of air that help move me along. My laptop bumps against my leg. By the time I reach the window, the sound of the sirens have died. I look around. In the dim light, I make out a wooden crate. The crate is just big enough to sit on. I plop myself down and open my laptop.

I turn it on and squint at the screen. The hot scene is there. I begin to type. The laptop slips. I reposition it against my knee. I write fast, real fast. I have to get the scene down before it slips away.

THE TACKLE BOX FILES

HER HUSBAND, ALBERT, is cranky today. He always is when his feet are swollen. He sits with them propped on a hassock, shoes untied, laces loose and dangling around his puffy ankles. Laura Lee, who is digging about in the extra refrigerator outside in the carport, doesn't know if the crankiness is from the swelling or vice versa. All she knows is that they come in twos and she's leaving today.

"Close the door, for Christ's sake. Were you raised in a barn?" he yells over the hum of the window unit in the family room.

"I can't," she yells back. "My hands are full." They aren't, but she says they are anyway. He knows where she was raised—five miles down the road on the Ridley Place.

"Then use your foot. Slam it closed."

"Would you calm down?"

"Not as long as you intend to air condition all of Crumb County."

"I'm coming inside right now."

"You always have to have the last word, don't you?"

"Not necessarily." With a jar of midget dills in one hand, a head of red cabbage in the other, she backs into the room. She winds up slamming the door with the tip of her toe after all.

Albert punches the remote and a fat lady in black tights pops onto the television screen. Groaning, she bends across a pendulous belly and bulging thighs to touch her toes. "Would you look at that?" he crows. "And I thought *you* had big legs."

Laura Lee reaches for the grater under the kitchen counter and acts as if she hasn't heard. She knows he's getting even, lets it pass. Instead she watches the shredded cabbage fall like confetti into the mixing bowl and thinks of Starling. At this minute, he's in town at Sports Unlimited buying a motorcycle helmet for her.

"You'll pick up an extra one of those," she'd said this morning as he pulled on his helmet and mounted the Harley. In her mind's eye she pictures the two of them winding down the blacktop together, their helmets bobbing like party balloons. When he looked up at her and smiled, Laura Lee knew he was taking her with him.

Two weeks earlier, Starling's bike had careened off the road in front of the house and shuddered to a stop astride their deep well pump. With his eyes squinted against the white hot sky, he'd picked himself up, unhurt. Behind him, the Harley lay bent like a crippled animal.

When Albert saw the damage, he said he felt responsible. Laura Lee didn't understand why. Since he's been sick, the way he looks at things sometimes makes no sense to her. At first she wondered if he was confused. The doctor had said this could happen, but she's decided it's more a matter of flawed logic.

"After all, it is our pump," he explained, which as far as she was concerned didn't explain taking a complete stranger into their home.

So Starling wound up installed in the spare bedroom to wait for parts while Laura Lee stood in the doorway holding in her stomach as hard as she could.

Albert flips off the television set now. "Do I get something to eat today?"

He's seen the pickles and cabbage, so he doesn't need to ask. Not a day goes by that he's not fed—and well, too. In fact, she loves to cook. Chopping settles her down better than a Xanax. The comforting feel of the knife handle seated in her palm, the crisp snap of the blade, the repetitive back and forth dissolves the tight knots of resentment that flare up and frighten her. Cooking takes the place of the words she needs to say and can't.

"We'll eat as soon as I finish the coleslaw," she says.

"You expect me to live on nothing but air and water like a tree." He munches the words, spits them out like breadcrumbs. Then his lips cave in. His teeth are out. He's probably left them in the bathroom again.

"When you depend on someone else to do things for you, you sometimes have to settle for less than perfect," she says, then reminds herself if she wanted a husband who wasn't prickly and full of complaints, she needed to be married to someone else.

She dries her hands on a dishtowel and thinks of Albert as a tree. His plump arms cross his sturdy drum chest and he sits immovable. His gray hair is pushed up on one side of his head where he's slept on it wrong. Matted curls climb in tangles down his neck along with the oxygen tube that tethers him like a leash. He could use a haircut.

In the bathroom, his teeth sit balanced on the edge of the sink. She cups them in a Kleenex and lifts them gingerly. Lots of things she does without thinking—sorting laundry, defrosting the freezer—but handling Albert's dentures with a naked hand isn't one of them.

She inches quietly up to his chair with the teeth behind her. He eyes her for a second, his Adam's apple bobbing up and down, then says, "Okay, fork 'em over."

Laura Lee cradles them in the Kleenex and serves them to him like a highball on a drink tray. He pops them into his mouth, then smacks his lips and grins. He knows how she detests touching them; he forgets them on purpose.

At the sink, she eyes the *Love is Blind* sign centered in a red Valentine heart on the refrigerator door, a cereal box prize. She remembers a time when this was true, when she and Albert fit together perfectly. Like a jigsaw puzzle, he filled in her missing parts and she did the same for him. But this was before she found the pictures, before she began to run away, before Starling. She reaches over and tilts the heart upright. It still adds a nice splash of color to the spartan white.

She slides the cabbage against the grater and her finger inadvertently scrapes against a rough strip of metal along its bottom. Before she can staunch the blood, it wells from the cut and drips into the bowl, mixing with the red cabbage. She glances at Albert. He dozes with his head lolling against the back of the chair. She tosses the shredded cabbage about in the bowl and blends the reds together. Honest to God, if it's anything she hates, it's keeping track of his teeth.

The cut on her finger has almost stopped bleeding. She bandages it, then struggles to open the lid on the pickle jar. In addition to the cut finger, her hands ache and their joints are stiff. Once her fingers were so nimble, she'd taught little Sammie Stringer, who couldn't find his way home alone in a rainstorm, to debone a chicken so skillfully the skin fit taut as a rubber glove over the meat. Now she has trouble unscrewing the lid from a jar of midget dills.

Laura Lee wonders if Starling is bothered by arthritis. She's heard everyone over forty is troubled by it. He's forty-one, nine years younger than she. At sixty-five, Albert suffers terribly from it. "Some mornings I creak like the tin man," he tells her.

Starling is tiny, smaller than Albert, so maybe he's less affected by arthritis. She smiles, thinking of his thin mustache that quivers when he talks—which isn't much. He tries to be unobtrusive, but she feels Starling behind her, watching her from a doorway even when he doesn't speak.

She rests the pickle jar on its side in the sink, then taps it with a knife handle. The jar breaks, cracking open like an eggshell.

"What's going on over there?" Albert asks.

"I'm opening a jar of dills."

Laura Lee rinses a pickle under the faucet, then leans across the lazy Susan on the counter and dangles the pickle in a silly pickle jig. Albert laughs first, then she chuckles. With her hips swaying, she spins across the kitchen toward him, the pickle twirling like a castanet over her head.

When Albert coughs, choking on his laughter, she stops and reaches for his pill bottle on the windowsill. As she does, her eyes are drawn to the two weeping willows outside. Their branches sweep in circles like hoop skirts caught in the wind. Albert had planted them the first year they were married after they'd caught her fancy at White Rose. She remembers standing at this window and watching him at work, the handsome knot of muscles rippling across his back, his skin slick with sweat. When they were set firmly in the ground, he'd turned and saluted her with a grin.

Rushing outside, she'd smothered him in kisses. "Stand still," she'd ordered while he squirmed. "I'll be done in a jiffy."

He tried to hide his smile, but Laura Lee knew he loved that she didn't hold back. He was the one with few words and she, the loudmouth, who never waited for him to say I love you. But he adored her chatter and the silly things she said to make him laugh. "They're what made me fall in love with you," he said.

One day, when he was so quiet she wanted to shake him, he asked, "I don't say it much, but you do believe I love you?"

Studying him for a moment, she replied, "As much as you're capable of loving anyone."

"My capacity for loving you amazes even me."

And that's when she fell in love with him.

Glancing down at the bowl of cabbage now, the red streaked with the darker burgundy, she hesitates. She pictures Albert's broad smile that brimmed with hope. How proud and manly he looked standing beside the weeping willows while dandelions cartwheeled around him. She dumps the cabbage into the disposal.

For a second she'd forgotten Albert's pills. Now his hacking cough brings her back to the moment. She shakes a pill from the bottle into her palm, adding an extra one for the swelling in his ankles. If he takes it now, he won't be back and forth all night to the bathroom.

As he swallows the pills, she runs her hands down the side of her legs and over the creases in her new jeans. The hands might be a little stiff, but the rest of her is in splendid shape. Her thighs are firm, a tad heavy, she admits, and there's a slight thickening at her waist. In fact, she's worn a girdle since Starling showed up. She tries to hold in her stomach but has a tendency to forget. The jeans are for the Harley, of course. She bought them on sale yesterday at The Gap.

"Did they go down?"

Albert nods. He never uses water for the pills anymore. He's taken so many, he's learned to collect saliva on the back of his tongue and washes them down with that.

She hears a sound outside and looks up to see if it's Claude, Albert's brother. He lives in the farmhouse next door and drops by every morning to check on Albert. The two of them are close. Albert will be fine whether she's here or not.

The sound she'd heard was a pickup rattling past. As she turns back, her eyes linger for a moment on the ivy crowding the porch rail. She hates how this spring the vine has choked out the morning glories; not a speck of blue is to be seen.

Since Albert wouldn't let Starling pay to stay with them, he looked for things to do to help out. The barbequed chicken he cooked on the grill turned out dry and overly sweet, and he couldn't tell a weed from a carrot in her garden. Finally she sat him on a stool at the kitchen counter, poured him a cup of coffee and said, "Talk to me while I work.. Tell me about yourself."

She learned he'd once taught American history at a Blue Ridge high school, he'd worked on a tree farm in Blackshear, and he'd spent a summer in Jordan tutoring a sheik's son, a little boy with a lisp who sprayed Starling consistently with spit. She laughed then and he did too, setting his thin black mustache aquiver.

Yesterday, after two weeks of waiting, the part for the Harley arrived. When the bike was fixed, Starling took her for a ride. In the driveway, he revved the motor until the bike trembled beneath them like something alive. Then he whipped onto the two-lane.

She sat on the seat behind him with her hands clasped around his waist. He kept glancing around, as if checking to make sure she was still there behind him.

Resting her cheek against his back, Laura Lee listened to insects pop against the windshield. She'd never been on a motorcycle before. She was amazed at how close she was to the glittering mica stretched in front of them. When the wind tugged at her short hair, she suddenly wished she hadn't listened to Maude at the beauty parlor. "Nobody over forty should wear long hair," she'd said. What did Maude know? Recklessly, Laura Lee tossed her head and imagined her hair whipping out behind her.

"You'd like my cabin in North Carolina," he said after the bike ride. "It's on a ridge overlooking the Parkway, so high up not a power line in sight. In the evening, the sinking sun lights on the wild azaleas, setting the whole side of the mountain on fire."

From the look he gave her, Laura Lee knew she was there with him in his mind.

Eleven years ago last spring, she and Albert spent a week in the mountains. It rained the entire time. Fierce wind and rain swept against the thin cabin walls, sealing them inside like clams in a shell. Restless and sullen at the rain and the desolate cabin, Albert cursed, "I'll shave when I see the goddamn sun again and not before." He'd spent the week fiddling with his new camera, one which had a tripod and timer.

They saw the sun again in Macon on the drive home. By that time, his face was covered in hair as stiff and wiry as a Brillo pad.

"Oh, hon, I like your beard." She leaned against him, remembering the crack of the thunder and the hot ozone smell of lightning that flashed and lit up the cabin. Her blood, which felt sluggish in the humid low country, raced bold and energetic in the mountains. "It's like being married to Long John Silver," she said.

He shaved off his beard anyway.

Two weeks later, she found the pictures.

* * *

When Sol Flick at the post office said redbreasts were biting at the millpond, Laura Lee thought of her yellow-speckled lure. Redbreasts would strike at it when they'd swim past anything else. She'd taken it with her to the mountains, but couldn't find it in her toolbox. Albert rarely borrowed her lures—*mine catch more fish than yours any day*, he claimed—but maybe it had wound up in his box by mistake.

Yes, there it was beneath his extra spools of line and under it, the file folder with the pictures. Puzzled, she pulled out the first photo and held it up, confused at what she saw. The disembodied figures, the stark bare flesh. Witness to a bank robbery once, she remembers this element of surprise and the moments of free-fall confusion while she grasped what was happening. Later she thought often of that moment, how her stunned mind had grappled for meaning.

Finally, when she recognized the two people in the picture, the significance of the bare back and naked leg, her own legs folded like an accordion beneath her. She slumped to the floor, the folder clutched to her chest. In the distance, the putt-putt of a tractor broke the quiet and mingled with the smell of newly tilled earth. Someone had bought the old Samson place and was plowing the meadow for planting. Overhead a mourning dove fluttered, busy building a nest in a basket of wandering Jew. The plant's purple leaves were so dark, they looked black against the white shingled wall. She marveled at the sounds, the smells, the rich contrast of colors while a low moan that started at the tips of her toes worked itself up through her body.

The folder contained eight pictures scattered about behind the letters of the alphabet. Behind the letter *A* was a picture of Albert and Ann Smithers. Even with her face half hidden, Laura Lee recognized the bobbed haircut and Albert's hand spread like an opened fan across her stomach. His father's signet ring looked thick and heavy against Anne's delicate bare skin.

Filed behind the letter B was a picture of Albert and Barbara Lester, one of the twins, who worked at the Twilight Boutique where Laura Lee had discovered the iced tea pitcher with butterflies etched in the glass.

She held her breath and sped through the early letters of the alphabet. Finding no more photos, she skipped ahead hopefully, but her hope died at the shocking snapshot behind the letter T. Laura Lee thinks of how scared she was in first grade and how Maggie Harris, the woman in the photo who was a year older and in second, had taken her hand. "I'll go with you," she said, and they'd climbed the schoolhouse steps together. The week before, Maggie had sat at Laura Lee's kitchen table with her bra strap showing and sobbed about how if she didn't catch a man soon, she'd surely wind up an old maid. Distracted by a weird-sounding recipe in the new *Southern Living* that mixed watermelon with bleu cheese, Laura Lee said dismissively, "Honestly, Maggie, you and your drama. Have another piece of sponge cake."

In the picture, Maggie lay beside Albert, her freckled skin naked and conspicuous against the lap robe stretched beneath them. Behind them, Laura Lee made out a tumbled down fence similar to the one at the Pinkney Place on Millcreek Road. A single huge sunflower tilted against Maggie's leg, its face turned to the sun. Maggie was a sight without clothes. Laura Lee could see why she hadn't had any takers.

Suddenly she was seized by an outrageous need to laugh out loud. She covered her mouth with her hand, capturing the bizarre sound before it could escape. Did being someone's mistress knock Maggie out of the old maid category? Laura Lee certainly hoped not. The spiteful thought left her light-headed and giddy with a grainy taste on her tongue.

The last photo behind the letter Z was mostly shadow. Even in the dim light, she recognized Albert's leg, she'd know it anyplace, but the other parts of the picture were deep in shadow. Was that the head of a bed? Perhaps an open window? Someone's arm? She could make out long hair fanned against a pillow with a face just out of the frame.

Laura Lee turned the picture back and forth in the light, searching. Finally she gave up. She returned it to the tackle box along with the other photos and closed the lid. The heat of the day had faded and a moist chill crept through her, numbing her fingertips, her feet. Cold seeped from the damp concrete through her jeans and into the backs of her legs, and a heavy lump lay like a bruise in her chest.

In the family room, she wrapped an afghan around her stiff knees. Closing her eyes, she relived over and over again the moment she'd looked at the first photo. What she hated most about knowing was that once she knew, she could never not know again.

In bed at night, she'd practiced what to say to Albert, but the words she came up with never seemed quite right.

Laura Lee stretches on tiptoe to replace the pill bottle in the windowsill. Albert watches her and the snug fit of the jeans, the soft bulge at her waist. She knows what he's going to say before he says it.

"You know something, Laura Lee? Some people shouldn't wear jeans."

"Oh?"

"*You* are one of those people." He points his finger at her. Then he runs his hand down his pants leg, mocking her.

Last night while she turned down their bed, he'd shuffled to the bedroom door. "I'm supposed to be dead now, you know."

"Albert, please! I hate when you talk like that."

"You'd like that, wouldn't you?" he said, leering at her from the doorway. "For me to be gone?"

Last spring during a bad time, Dr. Deak told them Albert wouldn't last through Christmas. She thinks of his life, a life spent being in control. Now he needs help getting out the front door. How that must feel, she can't imagine. She swears he's staying alive now for spite, to prove the doctor wrong. Who says being stubborn and determined isn't a good thing?

"Doctors don't know everything," she said. Before Starling arrived, she often wondered what Albert would say if she replied, "You're right. I can't wait until you're gone." Now most often his baiting seems petty and insignificant.

Today the wait for Starling to come from town has left her edgy. She finds it hard to resist taking Albert's bait.

Six months after she found the pictures, Laura Lee ran away for the first time with a cotton farmer from Cordele. He'd stopped to ask for directions one July morning while Albert was in Metter at an all-day meeting on soil conservation. What broad shoulders he had for someone so short; his handsome fingers she found remarkably provocative. She imagined him playing the piano, his slender fingers, long and tapered, moving across the keys. She noticed his limp, but only later when he removed his trousers, did she see his twisted clubfoot.

They parked on Broughton in Savannah and traipsed hand in hand down the riddle of cobblestones to River Street. Laura Lee's blue silk dress, the one that brought out the color of her eyes, whispered against her thighs as she tripped along, her feet as dainty as a ballerina's, he said. With his hand guiding her firmly by the elbow, Laura Lee felt courageous and beautiful.

A crowd of people was gathered at the river where the bank sloped toward the water. Laura Lee and the farmer moved closer to see two black men drag a huge fishing net in the deep water slightly off shore.

"The baby's down on the bottom somewhere," muttered an old lady with smoky black skin. "Right there's where the woman pitched him in. Hauled off and slung him in like he was a bag of Dixie Crystal."

Suddenly, the hand that had guided Laura Lee with such assurance was gone. The spot on her arm felt bare and cool as though she'd thrown back the covers on a hot summer night and the breeze had chilled her skin.

Then a roar exploded behind them. The net had caught. Slowly the body of the dead baby emerged. Its arms were flung wide and marsh grass clung like soft putty to the mottled fingers. Dazed, she watched a solid mass of women hurtle toward her. At first she thought they were after her, but they were going for the dripping body of the baby.

"Take me home!" Laura Lee screamed at the cotton farmer.

In September, when the cloying heat of summer ended and the brisk days of fall began, she realized she was pregnant. Her nights became a kaleidoscope of flashing scenes—a baby dripping with marsh grass, huge grasping hands pulling her toward dark water, the memory of the man and an empty spot on her elbow.

The baby arrived in April when crepe myrtle blossoms hung from their branches like clusters of purple grapes. She was perfectly formed with Albert's dimple etched like a thin curved sickle in her chin and the umbilical cord wrapped so tightly around her neck, she never gasped once for air. They named her Virginia after Albert's mother and buried her in the family cemetery at the top of the hill. Laura Lee planted moss roses at the headstone and dusty miller at the foot of the grave. Then, like matting on a splendid painting, she framed it with row upon row of blazing salvia. Many mornings before dawn, she stood at the graveside pondering the notion of whether one's life is lived in separate compartments or if the events meld into one.

Five years later, she ran away again. This time she took off with an auto mechanic from Baxley who wore a belt buckle shaped like a tow truck. After a week, she came home. Perched on the hood of a car while the mechanic replaced brake shoes on a Chrysler Imperial wasn't exactly what she'd had in mind. It was her mistake, of course. She should have checked him out more carefully. Actually, all she'd done was make sure both his feet matched.

Albert had looked at her gravely when she hustled through the front door lugging her suitcase. She'd explained before she left that she'd be in Atlanta with Mary Dell Thompson, picking out flocked wallpaper for the living room.

Albert pushes the hassock away. He rises stiffly on his first trip to the bathroom—the pills at work. In the past year, he's lost weight and his cheeks are sunken. The wrinkled skin drapes in layers down his face. She watches him move sluggishly across the room. When his feet swell, his lungs fill, too. His breathing becomes raspy and cumbersome in his chest. It's a sound she's come to hate. Sometimes when it wakes her in the night, she pines to take Albert in her arms and whisper, "I am so afraid." If she did, would he bristle and pull away from her? Or would he relax and curl his body into hers? Before she can move, the picture of his hand on Ann's naked stomach pops into her head, so Laura Lee lies stone-still in the dark and listens to him struggle to breathe.

Have more pictures been added to the file folder? Perhaps there's one behind every letter of the alphabet now, like notches on a gun belt. She never opened the folder again. Instead she closed herself in silence and became as mute as he.

Laura Lee has no trouble opening the jar of mayonnaise. Whoever used it last didn't tighten the lid.

"What are we having with the coleslaw?" Albert asks.

"Chicken of the Sea."

"Again? Didn't we just have that?"

"Not since day before yesterday."

"It seems like that's all we have. Tuna! Tuna! Tuna!"

"In case you haven't noticed, Albert, this is not a restaurant."

"No, Laura Lee, I hadn't, but now that you've pointed it out to me. . .."

"Take it or leave it."

"Starling's gone and he's not coming back."

The mayonnaise jar slips. She catches it before it crashes to the floor. From the corner of her eye, she watches Albert. Finally, she says, "Oh, he'll be back."

"His shaving stuff is gone."

Laura Lee feels his eyes on her.

"I checked."

Behind her the refrigerator makes a noise, two sharp brittle squeaks close together that sound like a mouse. The noise started yesterday. Laura Lee figures if the mouse squeaks three times in a row, the refrigerator's gone. They'll need a new one.

She waits until Albert is absorbed in his television program. Then she edges toward the spare bedroom and slides open the closet door. A single wire hanger tilts at an angle on the clothes rack in the empty closet. She leans her head against the doorframe. The mountains must be breathtaking this time of year, the wild azaleas like flaming bouquets in the sinking sun. She can almost smell the fresh air, the intoxicating surge of energy that fills her when she leaves the low country. Shivering, she crosses her arms over her chest and hugs herself as the emptiness takes her. It spreads through her body like spilled water soaking into a carpet.

Suddenly she yearns for Ginny, born without the twisted clubfoot that would've been awkward for a little girl. She yearns for Starling, who was not deceived by the girdle after all. She yearns to be the woman in the photo behind the Z, the one with the long wavy hair.

Life is not a series of separate compartments, she's found, but one spilling over into the other like a nuclear waste leak. Did she really believe Starling would come back for her? Would she have gone with him if he had? Or does the fantasy of feeling she has a choice make staying easier?

She crosses the family room into the kitchen.

"Didn't I tell you he's not coming back?" Albert jeers.

Laura Lee stops. One, two, three, four, five . . . . Suddenly she spins. Flinging out her arms, she sweeps everything off the kitchen counter. The coffee maker goes flying. The lazy Susan bounces against the refrigerator door, then crashes to the floor. If anything was left on the counter to throw, she'd have it sailing across the room at Albert's head. With her hands on her hips, she turns and faces him. "I know about your nice little file folder of women, Albert. I found them a long time ago. So rather than complain about having tuna again, be thankful every sandwich I've made for you since then hasn't had poison planted in it."

Moving faster than she's seen him move in years, Albert jerks himself straight up in his chair, his mouth gaping. He looks so goofy with his mouth dropped open, she'd laugh—if she wasn't so furious. Instead, Laura Lee, who is normally not a crier, bursts into tears.

When Albert slides to the edge of his chair and tries to stand, she puts out her hand to stop him. Her words are strangled by sobs. "Those pictures just about killed me. My mistake was keeping them secret. Rather than fan them out like a deck of cards on the supper table and deal with them, I kept quiet and did shameful things to get back at you." Then, as quickly as her anger came, it leaves her. With the back of her hand, she swipes at her tears and says with a weary sigh, "Frankly, I'm sick to death of both of us."

Albert watches her silently.

"Now prop your feet on this stool to keep that swelling down. As soon as I take off this girdle, I'll fix us something to eat."

Lifting his feet, he places them on the hassock. Then he sinks back into the chair and studies her with an unfaltering gaze as if he's seeing her for the first time.

GOLDENROD

THE GREYHOUND BUS slid to a stop by the side of the road, its huge silver door easing open with a *hiss*. Perched high above like a king on a throne, the driver peered down, first at Mama, then at my brother Lee Ray.

"Lady, we're not equipped to handle afflicted people," he said. "If you can't find two seats together back there so that you can look out for him, you'll have to make other travel arrangements."

Before I could move, Mama's hand clamped down on my shoulder, anchoring me in place.

"We'll be fine," she said, making it sound like we really would.

Lee Ray leaned on his crutches; the armpits of his shirt dark with sweat rings. Centered on his head, sat the beanie cap he always wore. His red harmonica—named Pete for the man Daddy had bought it from—poked out of Lee Ray's shirt pocket, its wide silver stripe glinting in the late afternoon sunlight.

Lee Ray was twelve years old, a year older than I was. He was crippled from birth and couldn't talk or walk without help. What he could do was make music with Pete like you've never heard. When I played Pete, I sounded like a screech owl, but I walked and talked just fine—good enough for both Lee Ray and me.

When Mama was satisfied it was safe to let go of me, she said, "Here, Cherry, hold this." She passed her pocketbook across to me, then knelt and snapped the lock on Lee Ray's braces so his knees could bend. I watched while he dragged his feet through the sand toward the bus. What a struggle these trips were for him! Ordinarily, he'd have been in his wheelchair, but the Greyhound aisle was too narrow for it. This morning when we'd set out on our trip to see the faith healer in Lattimore, Mama had parked the wheelchair in the shady cove of sycamores where we caught the bus. A sparkle lit her eyes then, the shine I always saw when she was headed to another tent meeting to get Lee Ray cured—when this time for sure, her miracle was guaranteed to happen.

But that was this morning. Now on our way home in the late afternoon, Mama brushed back strands of hair limp from the heat and watched Lee Ray grapple for a foothold on the bottom step of the bus. With his lower lip caught between his teeth, he grabbed the edge of the door and pulled himself up, one step at a time. I was glad to see his mind on what he was doing. I never knew how much of what people said sank in with him. He couldn't seem to sift through the words and figure out what they meant. Sometimes he got mixed up and grinned whether the situation called for it or not. Then again, he could make Pete whine like a whirlwind or shriek like a wet setting hen, like he knew exactly what was going on and was trying to tell us about it. At times like that, I wondered if he understood more than I gave him credit for. Before he learned to play Pete, he made little groaning sounds when he tried to talk. Now Pete did Lee Ray's talking for him. Fair or not, whoever made the rules said he didn't get to play Pete and walk and talk, too.

I had a special gift, too. My gift was that I figured out things in a flash that took other people forever. It was like the feeling you get when somebody you care about is in trouble. You don't know how you know, but you do. I looked into people's minds and saw what they were thinking, before they came up with the thoughts themselves. I looked into their hearts and knew right away if they were good people out to do good or bad people set to do harm. Mama thought if you trusted people to do the right thing, nine times out of ten they'd do it, but my experience had proved otherwise.

One Sunday in Bible Study, I knew before Lucy Barlow cracked a smile that she'd point and snicker when Lee Ray walked jacklegged across the front of the room to his seat. Never one to sigh and throw up my hands over situations such as that, I stopped square in front of her so she'd know it was on purpose and stomped down as hard as I could on her Mary Janes. From the way she carried on, you'd have thought her toes were broken.

Of course, Mrs. Creasey, our Sunday school teacher I'd liked until then, told Daddy what I'd done.

"Cherry, you can tell yourself this is about Lee Ray, but the real reason you stepped on Lucy's toes is you never liked her in the first place and have been waiting for a chance to pick a fight," Daddy said. "Lee Ray was your excuse."

I couldn't have disagreed more. This was about following the rules. Mama and Daddy said they loved Lee Ray just the way he was and what other people thought about him didn't count, but I knew otherwise. If I was crippled and spastic and he was limber and spry and some smart aleck like Lucy Barlow laughed at me, I'd expect him to even the score. In fact, right now I was tempted to tell the bus driver, *Watch it, Mister, you don't have to talk to my mama like she's done something wrong just because her son needs help climbing the steps.* If I had something to puncture his tires with, he'd find one had suddenly sprung a leak. But the more I considered this, I realized if he had to stop and fix a flat, that meant Daddy would get home before we did. Today was cotton ginning-day and it would be a close call anyway. If he got home first, then he'd know Mama had taken Lee Ray to another faith healer. For that reason and that reason alone, I decided to *rise above* like Mama always told me to. "Your only duty, in a situation like this, is to have the good taste to keep your mouth shut," she'd say. So instead of saying anything, I smiled at the dandruff on the grouchy driver's shirt collar and developed a moving picture of a get-back-at-him in my mind. I envisioned him picking his nose when he thought nobody was watching, only to glance up and find everybody was. A feeble substitute I'll admit, but it would do for starters.

When Lee Ray reached the top step, Mama handed him his crutches and locked his braces. She watched him fit a crutch under each arm and move down the aisle. Once she was convinced he wouldn't fall, she took back her pocketbook and climbed the steps. At the top, she stopped for a second and glanced back over her shoulder like she was looking for someone. I didn't know who she was looking for, but I know who it wasn't and that was Daddy.

On the morning of his last trip to a faith healer with us, Daddy took forever to comb his hair at the bathroom sink. I knew his reason for dawdling. These trips to the different faith healers were Mama's idea. He'd just as soon stay home. They both said they accepted Lee Ray like he was; Daddy was the one who meant it.

After seeing the faith healer, Daddy had driven the truck home with a face like stone. He'd wheeled into the front yard and stopped under the chinaberry tree. I'd turned eight in March and had just learned to unlock Lee Ray's braces without pinching my fingers. In the truck bed, I was propped beside him on a low stool with my foot pressed against the chair to keep it from scooting. Daddy switched off the motor and dropped his head on the steering wheel. The *ping, ping* of the cooling engine sounded loud in the deep quiet.

With my back against the cab, I faced the long oak-shaded lane we'd just driven up. When we'd passed the gate posts, stationed like sentinels on either side of the cattle gap, Lee Ray's head swayed in greeting, saying a friendly hello to them like they were his best friends.

After the smothered feeling of the tent meeting with its noisy crowd-racket, I breathed in the bigness of the pecan orchard extending along the side yard. The openness of the trees lifted the coat of sawdust and suffering we'd brought home with us.

When we'd sat for a second listening to the quiet, Lee Ray raised Pete to his lips. A moaning sound came out. It was like the echo of the freight train's whistle as it rounded the Satler Creek bend.

Suddenly Daddy hit the steering wheel with a sharp *thud!*

"No lunatic who calls himself a faith healer is ever going to lay another hand on Lee Ray as long as I live," he said. "I've driven my last mile chasing after something that's never going to happen."

When he hit the steering wheel, Lee Ray and I jumped like a gun exploding, but Mama acted like he hadn't uttered a word. "Cherry, go check the nests. See if those Rhode Island Reds have laid enough eggs for supper while we get this wheelchair out of the truck. If there's enough, I'll make us a nice omelette with fresh scallions and chocolate bread pudding for dessert."

I climbed out of the truck bed and went searching for the eggs. The hens scattered in the coop with a great flapping of wings, throwing up a fog of musky droppings. I held my breath to keep from choking. In the back of my mind, I wondered if Lee Ray knew why we took him to tent meetings. I was too little to know then, but later I found out that as a rule, deep down inside, people usually know—at least ordinary people do. With Lee Ray, it was hard to tell. He seemed the same riding into town as he did on the ride home—still grinning, still playing Pete and still crippled.

Mama turned now and followed Lee Ray down the aisle. I hopped up the steps behind her, totally ignoring the bus driver. I'd barely scooted inside before he closed the door with a final *swish*.

That makes two, I thought, and don't think I'm not counting.

Two little girls looked doe-eyed at us when Mama stopped Lee Ray at some empty seats across the aisle from them. As she helped him into the window seat, they covered their mouths with their hands and leaned as far away from him as they could.

"Cherry, I'll sit up here next to him. You take one of those seats." Mama pointed to two empty seats behind her.

I ducked under her arm and scooted into the window seat. If I was grading the empty-headed girls, they'd get a C minus.

Meanwhile Mama reached across Lee Ray and opened the window, then sat down beside him. Rummaging in her purse, she found a handkerchief and wiped a drop of spit balanced like a teardrop on his bottom lip. Then she patted his arm and pulled a book from her purse. On our ride into town this morning, she'd done this exact same thing. As soon as we were settled, she'd started reading, except this morning before she'd begun, she'd crossed the fingers on both her hands.

I stared at those fingers. Only once before had I seen them crossed like they were then. I thought of that time and how it never came to mind without making me feel like that awful thing was happening all over again.

Mama, Lee Ray and I had been on the front porch. Mama shelled snap peas while we watched Lee Ray try to hit his mouth with a spoon. I laughed at the cheerful fuss he made when he kept missing. After a while, Mama said out of the blue, "When I'm gone, Cherry, it'll be your job to take care of Lee Ray."

"Where are you going?" I asked. "I can't take care of Lee Ray. I'm too little. I don't know a thing about his braces. Who'll take care of me?" My words spilled out shaky, one on top of the other. Who'd help me? Not Daddy. He worked late, already coming in after dark every night during picking season. Never mind in high school when I discovered boys and basketball and he found time to ride the school bus to every game so he could keep an eye on me. I was so embarrassed! But that was later and about trust, which by then, he had none of—a time when Mama had taken Lee Ray and left and Daddy and I had come to think in a new way about the word *family*.

When Mama saw my face, she said, "Oh honey, I didn't mean to scare you. Forget what I said. I'm not going anyplace."

"Cross your heart and hope to die, you'll never never leave."

"Cross my heart and hope to die. And my fingers, too," she said, holding them up for me to see. "Now, go and swing Lee Ray while I set the supper table."

As I swung him back and forth, pushing him up and down, I talked to myself in my mind. Why can't I have a regular brother? I never even wanted a brother. I wanted a sister, but look what I got. I was so tired of making sure Lee Ray's shoes were tied so he wouldn't trip; I was so tired of having to get back at people when they laughed at him.

The harder I thought about what I had to go through for Lee Ray, the madder I got. It's just not fair! The madder I got, the harder I pushed. The swing flew up, up, up until his toes touched the porch ceiling. It scared me. I knew he could fall out and hurt himself and although something inside told me to stop, I kept pushing.

Suddenly, I felt Mama lift me from behind. She swung me into the air, then holding me against her, she reached around and stopped the swing.

I hid my face in her soft front and broke down and cried. When I'd cried myself out, I was too tired to lift my head. I rested against Mama until I felt a tap tapping on my arm. I looked up; it was Lee Ray. He was trying to tickle my arm. The more he tried, the more his hand wobbled, and the more his hand wobbled, the more he grinned.

This morning when I saw Mama's crossed fingers, I was reminded of that day and thought, honestly, when you're little you don't know diddly-squat. Of course, I'd take care of Lee Ray. That's what sisters are for.

On the bus now, I watched the two girls watch Lee Ray. From the way they kept staring after Mama had wiped his mouth, you'd have thought they expected him to slobber all over himself. I kept my eyes on them for a few minutes. Once satisfied they were up to no mischief, I turned toward the window and gave myself over

to the strange top-heavy rhythm of the bus. The upper part
swayed but the bottom held steady, like they were divided and I
was caught in the middle. So I sat back and gave myself over to
the funny, separated feeling between my upper and lower self.

This morning, once we reached the fairgrounds in Lattimore, we
didn't stick around long after seeing Brother Lehue. We didn't
need to; what happened didn't take long.

We were met with a sign outside the tent that said, *Known for
healing weak limbs and weak minds and various other maladies.* In person,
Brother Lehue turned out to be a short, sturdy man with fat
cheeks and a stream of booming words that ran together like a
loud mouth auctioneer.

Inside of the tent, Mama helped Lee Ray down to the front, the
egg money making a solid *clank, clank* when she dropped the coins
into the collection plate. I'd skipped breakfast this morning. With
my stomach growling, I walked behind them to make sure Lee
Ray didn't trip.

Mama's eyes kept their dewy finish until everybody else who'd
come for a cure had left the front of the tent, and Lee Ray still
leaned on his crutches. Then with her head lowered, she turned
and walked back up the aisle. She kept her head down, like she'd
lost something in the sawdust and was searching for it now. I
knew what she'd lost. She'd lost her special picture of Lee Ray, the
one she kept stored in her head—the one of him running and
jumping and playing like other little boys, the picture I'd had in my
head too, the one I had trouble bringing into focus now.

Lee Ray trudged behind in his thick shoes with their built-in
braces. I followed him, kicking up the sawdust, doing anything to
keep from turning around and spitting in Brother Lehue's face.
He'd earned himself a solid F. To block him out of my mind, I did
what I'd done so many times before. I tried to picture Lee Ray's
feet cramped up in his thick heavy shoes. Did his toes hurt? I'll
bet they felt imprisoned, bunched up together under the stiff

leather. With his shoes off, his toes looked joined together in lumpy knobs like tinker toys.

I wondered if Mama's miracle, when it happened, would change his feet into ordinary feet that ran and played in cool open-toed shoes that let his toes wiggle. Why, I'd bet it would. I'd bet the miracle she was counting on wouldn't stop with his toes. It would give him a whole new makeover. Then he'd glide about slick and smooth like Gene Kelley tap dancing in the rain. He'd sing like Perry Como rhapsodizing on *Amore*. Of course, he'd start to school then and turn out to be the smartest kid in his class. He'd brim with words boarded up inside of him for so long. He'd grow up, reverting at times to child- like activities he'd missed, fort building and playing shoot 'em up cowboys. Then he'd move to Atlanta where he'd make a killing at Coca-Cola—no dead end jobs for straight A Lee Ray. He'd buy our tickets up on the Nancy Hanks to see the Cyclorama so many times we'd lose track, then hand me the Sears and Roebuck catalog and say, *Order anything you'd like and I'll pay for it.* I'd say back, *Why, thank you very much, Lee Ray, I don't mind if I do.* My first choice would be the entire set of biography books with the orange covers, but Sears and Roebuck is short on books, except product manuals for the items they sell. I'd make do with that fancy blue dress with frills on page 152. Plus two of the Monopoly sets on 190, so when we lose the hotels in one we can still play. And the Swiss doll like Heidi on page 174 you don't play with, just set up on a shelf and look at, with a china face and eyes that blink.

I could hardly wait for this miracle to happen, my own spread-out toes tingling with the happiness of it all. Just like that, I had talked myself into believing again.

Outside the bus window, a solid line of loblolly pines banked the highway. With the swaying of the bus and the tree trunks flashing past, my head was spinning. I was about to look away when, in the reflection from the window, I saw the two lame-brained little girls across the aisle. One had slick black hair tied with a silk bow of a

199

churned butter color. The other's blue eyes were big as all day suckers and she was plump, with soft wrinkles of fat gathered at her elbows and wrists. They were still perched on the edge of their seats and had yet to take their eyes off Lee Ray. I couldn't imagine why. His beanie was tilted to one side and with his head balanced against the seat back, it hardly wobbled at all. If you didn't know better, you've have thought he was like everybody else as he slid Pete from his pocket and played a soft, wavering melody. Next to him, Mama's eyes drooped. The sound of the music and the hum of the bus made me sleepy. Before I knew it, I was dozing, too.

The bus turned a sharp curve and my eyes flew open. Sleep drunk, I pressed my head against the seat and tried to find something to focus on. What I found was the bus's rear view mirror and the driver staring me square in the face. Wide awake now, I snapped to with a fierce glare back, proving what some folks already knew—I'm famous for holding grudges. I held the meanness for a count of ten and listened to Lee Ray tone Pete down to a hum. Then I side-glanced across the aisle at the two girls. Suddenly, my cocksure manner failed and my stomach lurched.

The girl nearest the aisle had thrown back her head and a tiny drop of spit, so small it was hard to spot, glistened on her bottom lip. Reaching over, the fat girl wiped the spit from the other girl's lip, just the way Mama had wiped the spit from Lee Ray's lip. Then the two girls giggled, laughing so hard they caved in against each other.

I gritted my teeth. I was glad to see Mama had dropped her book and closed her eyes. I didn't want her asking, "Is what you're thinking of doing going to help or harm?" I gripped my seat to keep from reaching over and snatching every hair out of the girls' heads. If a rising-above situation was ever called for, it was now. I was so mad. I leaned toward the window to catch the breeze and set about manufacturing a proper get-back-at picture in my mind. The best I could come up with was a slide show of the girls prancing down the center aisle of the bus with their shorts caught in their cracks. I was working on a meaner version when Pete switched to a jumpy little tune with a rumble of close together toots. Before I knew it, the music had swooped down and caught me up in its beat. Peeping through the crack in the seat, I was about to poke Lee Ray in the ribs when I saw Mama's sleepy relaxed look crumple and dissolve. She'd seen the girls making fun of her, too.

Closing my eyes, I wished that I could take back from her what she'd seen. I couldn't, of course, so I turned toward the window and squinched my eyes tight together. I felt like I was waiting for something. I wasn't sure what, so I just hung on listening to Pete's frolicking music collide with the wait.

I opened my eyes just in time to see Pete fly past Lee Ray's nose and sail out the window. It zipped past so fast, I jerked back in my seat like my nose was the one that was almost clipped. Pete bounced once. Then it took a funny little nosedive and landed in a clump of goldenrod.

I sat, chewing my lip and watching a replay of Pete flying past again and again and again. Finally I looked at Mama. She sat with her mouth gaped open and her hand still poised in the air. She was as shocked as I was at what she'd done. Her hand fell and she started to cry. I knew what the strangled sobs tearing though her fingers felt like. When you cry that hard, it hurts coming out.

Lee Ray hadn't moved. He sat with his hands in front of his face. I couldn't bear to look at him or Mama. My face felt red, if you could feel a color, and flushed, similar to when I had measles before the rash broke out. I felt like a spotlight was focused on us, lighting up Lee Ray and Mama and me in front of everybody, the two little girls, the man across the aisle with the loopy smile and, of course, the bus driver. Sure enough, when I looked up, he was zeroed in on us. He didn't say a word. He didn't have to; my sinking heart told me he'd seen it all.

I looked down then, my gaze holding fast on the floorboards. I knew what he was thinking—because I was thinking it, too. *You're no better than I am. And your mama's not either.*

Breathing hard, I listened to Mama's dry, hurting sobs while the bus *thump, thumped* over the cracks in the pavement. With each thump, we traveled farther and farther away from Pete. I turned to the window and rested my head against the metal plate skirting the bottom of the glass. The cool dampness of the metal soothed the fire in my cheeks. The loblollies passed in a blur. That afternoon on the porch, I never had asked Mama about being scared. Now I didn't have to; now I knew being scared made you do things you wouldn't do otherwise.

After a few minutes of my sitting quietly, something about the bus suddenly changed. A new slower rhythm took over. The trees that had whizzed past before were barely moving now. I felt the bus slow, then stop on the shoulder of the road and begin backing up. Finally, it came to rest. Startled, I looked up to find the driver gazing back at me in the mirror.

"Make it snappy," he said and opened the door. "We're due in Lemon Springs in twenty minutes."

As if his words had flipped a switch, I sprang up and wiggled across the empty seat, then headed up the aisle. I took the steps in a giant leap and landed on the run. Dog fennel whipped my ankles and sand spurs tangled in the hem of my dress as I sped back down the highway.

I flew along, feeling that whatever kept me anchored, whatever let me walk around without floating off to the moon, had eased off some for this race. Just this once, it decided to let me run faster than I'd ever run before. I threw back my shoulders and let its powerful flow propel me forward. It lifted me through the layers of thick green air to Pete's song that called to me in a flash of silver.

When I reached the clump of goldenrod, I fished Pete out of his tangled nest. Then standing on my tiptoes, I threw up my hands as high as I could reach. The good feeling I had now and the pain I felt for Lee Ray would always be connected. But for now, with the bus waiting and Pete waving high above my head, the good feeling was all there was.

ACKNOWLEDGEMENTS

The publication of this collection of short stories marks thirty years of a writing life kept alive by the faithful cheerleading, support and encouragement of friends, family and colleagues. I greatly appreciate The Florida Department of Cultural Affairs, who honored my work with generous artist's fellowship grants in 1996, 2000 and again in 2010. My writer's groups, The Black Hammock, and The Write Group that included Geri Throne, Patrick Matthews, Julie Compton and Terri Chastain, worked tirelessly year after year to help make the stories better. A huge thank you goes to Peggy Abbott, who read the many versions of each story again and again, each time coming up with insightful and truthful—always truthful—suggestions. I am grateful to Rollins College and the wonderful community of Winter Park, Florida for their support of all things literary. I thank my many friends, who kept saying you can do this, you can do this, until I did. Lastly, I cherish most the love and support of my family, without whom my writing life would have never happened to begin with.

ABOUT THE AUTHOR

Linda L. Dunlap began her second career as a fiction writer in the late eighties after a successful career as a registered nurse. Her first story, "I'm Here, Mr. Sullivan," was published by *Pencil Press Quarterly* in 1987. Since then, she's had numerous short works published in literary and university presses across the country including *The Crescent Review, Florida Magazine, RE:AL, Timber Creek Review,* and *Savannah Literary Journal.* She was awarded artist's fellowship grants from the Florida Department of Cultural Affairs in 1996, in 2000 and again in 2010, and her short story, "Goldenrod" was nominated for a Pushcart Prize in 2010. A native of Georgia, she now lives in Winter Park, Florida and tries to write every day. Contact her at ldunlap@earthlink.net.

CPSIA information can be obtained at www.ICGtesting.com
Printed in the USA
LVOW11s1746291115

464580LV00002B/3/P